# NIGHTMARE
## THE NOVELIZATION

# MICHAEL GINGOLD

Based on the screenplay by Romano Scavolini

© Copyright 2023 by Severin Films Inc.
All Rights Reserved.

This is a work of fiction. Names, characters, business, events and incidents are the products of the author's imagination. Any resemblance to actual persons, living or dead, or actual events is purely coincidental.

First Edition

In association with Petulant Child Press

# BROOKLYN, NY-1978

**THE MAN'S NAKED** corpse was intact except for the three large stab wounds in his chest, and for his penis, which was missing.

It was that detail that made Louie Sabatella reel back a couple of steps, trying to keep down the pizza he'd eaten at Mayor Sal's just a half hour ago. Sal's made the best damn Sicilian in the neighborhood, and since he was going to be down here anyway, Louie figured he'd stop in and enjoy some before checking in on the family. Might as well get something out of the trip. This wasn't his job anyway; shouldn't the cops handle it if someone thought a loved one was missing? Or couldn't that someone come and check for themselves? But no, the alert came from a guy who lived in Rhode Island and hadn't been able to reach his brother in a few days, and the cops apparently had more important things to do in this part of town than look in on some people who might have just stepped out on an unexpected vacation.

So off Louie had gone to see what had happened to the upstairs residents of his building, which he always described as a two-family house even though the downstairs unit was really only big enough for one person. Some guy named George was in there, whom Louie hadn't seen since he moved in, but who always sent the rent check like clockwork and never complained about anything. Hell, that guy could disappear, or die suddenly in the apartment, and no one would probably notice for a while, until the rent was late, or the smell wafted upstairs.

But no, George wasn't dead, at least as far as Louie knew. But the man lying in front of Louie definitely was. And holy fuck, whoever did this must have had some serious personal grudge against the poor guy. It was one thing to kill him, but to cut off his . . . his . . .

*If the guy's name was Johnson, that would be appropriate, wouldn't it?* Louie pushed back against the thought the moment it popped into his head; it wasn't right to be joking to himself about this poor bastard and what had happened to him. But he couldn't help it; that's just what happened sometimes when he was faced with a terrible problem or situation. Humor was his "defense mechanism," was how his buddy Larry, who thought himself an amateur shrink, had put it. So no disrespect to this guy, and Louie was honestly horrified by what he was looking at . . .

Then he remembered that the guy's first name was Frank (-*furter! Wiener!*), and a smirk jumped onto his face before he could stop it. Okay, now was the time to get out of here before he lost it and call the cops. He didn't want to call from in here; he wanted to get back out into the rest of the world, where there were no mutilated bodies in his face . . .

The sight of blood seeping from under the closet door stopped him. He looked from the closet to the bed, and back. It couldn't be the man's blood, which was all over the bed and the carpet in front of it; the closet was on the other side of the room. Louie could have just bolted, and let the police discover where it was coming from, but some morbidly curious part of

# NIGHTMARE

him was compelled to find out for himself. Besides, what if whoever was in there was just badly injured, and needed his help? He went to the door, and slid it open.

Someone was in there, all right, but she was beyond saving. Frank's wife had apparently been roughly dropped onto the closet floor, splayed out amongst a bunch of shoes and a couple of fallen clothes. Her own clothes had also been stripped off, she had also been savaged in her chest with an apparently large blade, and she had also . . .

*Oh freakin' Christ!* Louie turned away, staggered to the open bedroom door, where he put a hand on the frame, steadying himself. Doing that to the man was one thing; he'd heard stories about similar things from his friend Dominic, who had connections that Louie didn't want to think about too much. But to do that to a woman? You'd have to be some completely around-the-bend sick-in-the-head fuck to carve up her . . .

*If their cat had been butchered too, that would be kind of a pun, right?* He didn't know where that thought came from, thought he was a pretty sick fuck himself for thinking it, and slapped himself, as if he could literally knock that terrible joke from his mind. Now was really the time to get out of here, but he only made it partway to the stairs before he stopped.

Something else had occurred to him: This couple did not, as far as he knew, have a cat, but they did have a daughter, a beautiful 13-year-old named Sheila. And he couldn't, just couldn't, leave here without confirming for himself that she was not dead, that she had in fact avoided the grotesque fate her parents had suffered. Because no one could be that sick, to ravage and kill someone so innocent, right?

He made his way down the hall, to the door of the

second bedroom. It was closed, and when he put his hand on the knob, he prayed silently that when he opened it, it would be just her bedroom, with the typical teen-idol posters on the walls and the typical pop albums on the shelves below a record player and the typical stuffed animals on the bed—the kind of stuff his own daughter had just recently grown out of. His prayer finished, he turned the knob and slowly pushed the door open.

To his great relief, no one was in there. Just a bed and a dresser and a clothes chest with a couple of drawers half-open and the posters and records he'd been expecting. No stuffed animals, though; Sheila must have outgrown those earlier than his Angelina had.

His eyes fell on the closet, and he felt compelled to check that, too. Just to be sure. It took the longest five seconds of his life to cross the room and slide the door open. But that was empty too, save for the hanging clothes and the jumble of shoes on the floor and an upper shelf piled high with board games and books and a couple of stuffed toys pushed toward the back—part of Sheila's past now. No Sheila, though, for which Louie felt a moment of gratitude. It was a small positive in the midst of all the horror he had faced.

Instead, he found her in the bathroom. He had just gone in there to splash some water on his face before heading out to report what he had found, and the temperature in the room seemed to drop about 40 degrees when he saw her small bare foot sticking out of the shower door. He didn't go any closer, and couldn't see much detail through the patterned glass of the stall, but he could make out enough. The pale skin of her nude body, her long, dark hair, patches of blood dried to an unpleasant brown.

## NIGHTMARE

*He must have gotten her parents while she was in the shower. That's why she didn't hear anything,* his mind raced to rationalize the situation. *Then he came in here and got her—unless maybe he killed her somewhere else in the house, brought her in here and took off her—*

Louie stopped his thoughts from going further. That was it. He took off down the hall, through the front room, to the door, threw that open, down the stairs toward the front door—

And stopped as he saw it was standing open.

He knew he hadn't left it that way. He always made sure to close doors securely behind him whenever he entered a building, one of his own or someone else's; the way the crime rate was in this city, you never knew who might try to follow you in. And he knew he had done so with this door. But now, there it was—not fully open, just enough for someone to slip in or out.

Someone who, he realized, could be responsible for the carnage he had just witnessed.

*But wait a minute, maybe it was the downstairs tenant—that guy George.* Sure, he had a key, it could have been him. But then, why would he leave the door standing open?

Maybe he intended to leave quickly. Maybe he just needed to grab something from his place and then hurry back out.

*Then why is there no sound coming from downstairs? And while we're at it, how could he not be aware of what went on in the apartment right above him?*

Well, maybe it happened when George was out. He's spent a day and a night or maybe two or even three unaware of the ghastly crime scene he was sharing the building with. Stuff like that happened all the time, though not as violently; an old person living alone would pass away in their bed or in front of the TV, and the neighbors wouldn't notice for a week or sometimes more until that funny smell started making its way into their spaces. Yeah, it was completely reasonable that George didn't know.

Then why was Louie so reluctant to call out George's name?

The silence from below was becoming deafening. From where Louie stood on the steps, he couldn't see down the lower stairwell to George's front door. Couldn't see whether it was open or closed. Couldn't tell if George was waiting there, after returning to the scene of the crime for whatever reason and discovering someone else was there—for surely he had heard Louie's footsteps on the old building's creaky floors—and was lurking with a knife, maybe the same one he had used to butcher that poor family, ready to leap out and attack the moment Louie came into his view . . .

Louie could have run back up to the family's apartment, slammed and locked the door, and called the police from there. But then, he thought, George—and now there was no doubt in his mind that George was the culprit—could come up and break down the door, and then Louie would be trapped in there with a madman coming after him.

The daylight just beyond the half-open front door beckoned. Louie carefully made his way down the stairs, doing everything he could to keep even the slightest creak from escaping. He was a couple of steps from the bottom when he was able to look over the railing and down into the lower residence.

That door stood ajar too. Beyond it, only one light was on, in the tiny kitchen, and in its meek glow Louie could see a phone mounted on the wall, as if tempting him.

Then a shadow fell across the phone. Louie fought the urge to scream and bolted out the front door. He pulled it shut behind him, for whatever that was worth, and ran faster than he had ever run in his life toward Roma's Deli on the corner.

# NEW YORK CITY—1981

**THE DREAMS ALWAYS** played out the same way, no matter which one it was. He would be looking at himself, and yet it was like he was seeing through his own eyes. It made no sense—how could he be doing both at the same time? But that realization only came to him once he was awake, and the nightmare was slowly dissipating from his mind. When he was in the midst of them, he was not in control of his thoughts. Dr. Williamson helped sometimes, and so did the drugs—but only to a certain extent. Once he went to sleep, his mind took over and plagued him with the awful sights over and over, as if his own brain had turned against him and become his enemy.

And even after suffering them dozens—hundreds?—of times, it was always like he had never experienced them before when he was in the midst of the dreams. He didn't know, couldn't see how they would end, and then they would come to their awful conclusion and he would shriek, just shriek uncontrollably, as if a small part of his psyche recognized where he was and what was happening and was trying to jolt him out of his slumber.

He was having one of those dreams right now, and this was an especially disconcerting one, because in it, he was lying in bed, tossing and turning, and he was watching his own sleep being disturbed. Suddenly he woke up, drenched in sweat, gasping as he recovered from whatever horrific fantasy had plagued him.

As he relaxed, he sensed something strange, and looked down at his sheet-covered legs. Something felt sticky and uncomfortable down there, and for a moment, he felt a sense of residual shame, an uncontrollable echo of those times as a boy when he had woken up to a sticky feeling inside his pajamas, and had to hastily but quietly run to the bathroom and clean himself up so his parents wouldn't find out what he'd done. Then he realized this wasn't the same thing; the stickiness was all over his legs and feet, and though he dreaded what he'd see, he knew he had to pull back the sheet to see what it was.

When he saw it, it made him cry out again in utter terror. The lower half of the bed was soaked in bright crimson blood, and strewn with severed body parts. Arms and legs and parts that were less discernable, all oozing gore and emitting a horrible smell of death that suddenly permeated the room. At the foot of the bed lay the severed head of a woman, one he vaguely thought he recognized, but couldn't identify.

He wanted to leap from the bed and escape the room, but he couldn't. He was unable to move, the shock having robbed him of any control over his own body, and all he could do was continue to scream.

Then the woman's eyes opened, and the look in them was not dead but very much alive, alive and staring straight into his own eyes, wordlessly accusing him. The mouth said nothing but the eyes said, with horrible clarity, *You did this to me* . . .

And that was always the point when he woke up, still screaming.

\*\*\*

## MICHAEL GINGOLD

George Tatum thrashed in his wheelchair, against the straitjacket that bound him, against the remnants of the nightmare still lingering in his mind, his tortured cries filling the small room. It was late, very late, and so it took a little while before anybody responded.

Eventually the red door that stood like a warning sign against the otherwise white wall opened, and two men in green scrubs entered. One immediately reached into a pocket and produced a small vial and hypodermic, filling up the syringe with clear liquid. The other pulled back the top of the straitjacket, far enough that his partner could give George his injection. George began to calm, his screams replaced by heaving gasps that gradually quieted.

Once he was under control, one of the men went to a small sink against a wall and came back with a glass of water. The other took out a small bottle of pills, dropped two into his hand and fed them to George, who took them weakly, followed by a drink from the glass. His breathing slowly neared normal, and the men stepped back, watching George as if waiting to see if the calm would only be brief. When it became clear the drugs had done their job, they left the room.

Had George been cognizant of anything, he might have heard one of the men say, "Gotta tell you, they're gonna have to give me a raise if I'm gonna . . . " before the door swung shut, cutting him off. Instead, George's mind was in a pleasant place, numbed to everything—including, blissfully, the fear . . .

# THE FIRST NIGHT
# COCOA BEACH, FLORIDA

**K**ATHY MORRISON LAY on the floor of the Temper family's TV room, reading a magazine while watching the tube, as she often did when she babysat there. For Tammy, at 11 the oldest of the three Temper kids, bedtime was 10 p.m., which meant that Kathy didn't get to relax till then. And there wasn't much on of interest at that time, so she put the news on mostly as background as she flipped through the latest *Cosmopolitan*.

Every so often, a story would come on the broadcast that would distract her from reading the makeup tips, like one tonight about the impending satellite launch at Cape Canaveral. The kids were excited about it, and Kathy had to admit she was too; launches like that were commonplace on the Space Coast, but even at 18, she still had a childlike enthusiasm for them.

Right now, though, the weather was on, which didn't interest her; it was February in Florida, not too hard to predict what that was going to be. So she was immersed in an article called "The Fiscal Facts of Living With a Man" when Tammy's voice came wailing down from upstairs.

# MICHAEL GINGOLD

"Kathy, come up here right now! Kathy!"

So much for a peaceful rest of the night—not like such a thing happened often in this house. But maybe, Kathy thought, she could nip this one in the bud by being firm from the start.

"Shut up!" she yelled back. "Good night!"

For a few moments, she thought that had done the trick. Then, Tammy again:

"Oh, Kathy, please!" Now joined by her sister Kim: "Kathy, please hurry, come up here, we need you!"

Kathy fell back onto the floor, eyes closed, fighting her growing exasperation. Did it have to be like this every time? For a little while, after she had started taking these jobs at the Tempers', everything had gone relatively smooth. The kids had been no more rambunctious than any others she had looked after, there was quiet after they went to bed, and the money their mother Susan paid was good. Then there was that one time back in October, and since then, every night at the Tempers' was an exercise in frustration. Only the good money had kept her from quitting.

*If only Susan would get back soon*, Kathy thought, but she knew it was not to be. She didn't even have to look at her watch. The weather was just ending and would be followed by sports, and then the news would be over, which meant it would soon be 11 p.m., and when Susan was out with Bob, she rarely got in before midnight on Friday nights, sometimes staying out till 1 or beyond. At first, Kathy appreciated the lateness of their carousing—more hours, more money. Now, she just wanted Susan to show up already so she could go home.

Instead, she got to her feet and went upstairs. The little voices continued: "Kathy! Hurry, please!"

"Shut up, I'm coming!"

# NIGHTMARE

She came up to the second floor, went to the girls' room, and opened the door, resisting the urge to throw it open. Inside, Tammy was sitting up in their big bed while Kim, a year younger but otherwise the spitting image of her sister, lay beside her, both looking frightened.

"Kathy, I saw somebody looking in the window at us," Tammy implored, and Kim added, "Me too!"

Immediately, Kathy knew what was going on, and she had no interest in playing out this game. She went to the window, and barely even looked outside before telling them, "There's nobody there. Nobody. Would you please, please go to sleep? For me, at least?"

They responded with silence, still looking genuinely scared. Softening her voice, Kathy said, "We're on the second floor, there's no way anyone could be looking in at you. Just turn out the light, close the blinds, and go to sleep, okay?"

Tammy nodded, and she and Kim drew the blinds over the windows behind their bed before settling in under the covers. "Good night," Kathy said, turning out the light and closing the door.

Downstairs, she settled in front of the TV with her magazine, waiting for the sports report to be over and the Late Movie to come on. Maybe it would be something good to distract her while waiting for Susan's return.

She didn't notice the pale face that loomed outside the living room window behind her, leering in at her. It moved closer to the glass—then withdrew as Tammy and Kim appeared at the bottom of the stairs.

"Kathy, I can't sleep!" Kim said. "Can I watch television with you?" "Me too?" Tammy seconded.

Kathy rolled over, not even wanting to stand. "Do you know what time it is? Would you please go to bed?"

## MICHAEL GINGOLD

Changing the subject—a trick she had already learned at her young age—Kim implored, "Kathy, do you know what time my mom will be home?"

"No, I don't know when she's coming home. Now go!" Kathy said, firmly enough to let them know there'd be repercussions if they disobeyed. Reluctantly, the girls headed back up to their room. Kathy waited for the sound of their door closing, smiled and went back to her reading.

Then came another sound, from outside. Like someone was creeping around the house. She looked up, waited . . . and there it was again. She really wanted to ignore it, but investigating unfamiliar sounds outside was part of the job description. You never knew . . .

Kathy put her sandals on and went to the side door. Opening it, she peered outside. Now was the moment in the movies, she thought, when she was supposed to yell, "Is someone there?" But anyone who would be there would be either friendly, and thus immediately show themselves, or some kind of peeper, in which case they obviously wouldn't respond. So instead, she narrowed her eyes, trying to see into the shadows cast by the streetlight on the corner. There wasn't much ground between the house and the street, and Kathy saw nothing there.

She stepped outside, went around to the front of the house. More shadows, and nothing else. Still, she had the sense that there was something else out here, something besides the darkness and the low trilling of frogs and insects. Somebody around, very close by . . .

Another sound came from above and behind her. She whirled, looked up—and what she saw made her cry out in fear . . .

\*\*\*

# NIGHTMARE

About fifteen minutes later, a police officer emerged from an upstairs window of the Temper house, and with his flashlight scanned the portion of the roof where Kathy had seen the face. No sign of anyone, and he wasn't surprised. This wasn't the first false-alarm call they'd answered at this address.

He called down to his partner: "I don't see a damn thing up here."

The other cop, an older man with a resigned look on his face, called back: "OK, come on down." He got into their car and picked up the radio. "We can't find anything out here . . ."

In the house, Kathy sat with Susan, getting herself under control. Susan had arrived just before the cops got there to find her babysitter distraught and on the verge of tears, but as far as she could tell, Kathy had just suffered a momentary fright. And after what Susan had just overheard from outside, there was nothing to be concerned about.

"Did you hear that?" she asked Kathy. "The cops didn't find anyone."

"I know what I saw!" Kathy exclaimed. "It was a face, a man's face. He was staring at me! And the girls saw him too."

"Now, how could a grown man be running around on the roof without you hearing him?"

"I don't know. I had the TV on, maybe that's why!"

"Look, maybe it was just C.J. playing one of his pranks. I'll talk to him tonight."

"Even if it was him, you know he won't admit it. He'll just lie like he always does."

"Kathy, that's not fair. Maybe if you'd treat him more like . . ."

"Like what? Like he's a normal kid? He's not normal, Mrs. Temper. He needs help."

## MICHAEL GINGOLD

"I think I know what's best for my son," Susan said, trying not to sound too harsh toward Kathy, who was still clearly upset. She reached for her purse, took out Kathy's money plus an additional ten. "Here, a little extra for you. I'll drive you home now."

Kathy took the money and stood up abruptly. "No thanks. I'll walk."

"Nonsense, let me take you."

"I'd really rather just . . . be by myself for a little while."

"But it's so late. And it's dark out there."

"It's less than ten blocks. And there are lights." She made for the door, then turned halfway across the room. "Besides, there's no one out there, right?"

"Kathy . . . " But then she was gone. Susan sat for a moment, and let out a long breath. The night had gone so well, she and Bob had had such a good time, and then she'd come home to this. She would have that talk with C.J.—but not now. It was late, he was in bed asleep and she wanted to get to her bed as well.

She didn't notice C.J. standing in the darkness a few feet back from the top of the stairs. The nine-year-old had watched the whole thing, an evil little grin creeping across his face, and he covered his mouth to stifle a laugh. The prank had worked perfectly, and the creepy mask and the wooden pole he'd mounted it on were safely hidden away. It was so easy to scare Kathy—he'd learned that in October, when he'd left the rubber snake in the bathtub for her to find when she went in to take a shower. After enduring her scolding, he'd quietly laughed himself to sleep over that one.

Susan stood up, and C.J. retreated back down the hall, slipping into his room and into his bed. Lying in the darkness, he was already thinking about his next prank.

# NEW YORK CITY

**THE WORST DREAM** tended to come in fragments, as if his mind was teasing him, or perhaps there was a part of it trying to protect him by not showing him everything. But he always saw enough, every single time.

He saw himself coming up the stairs outside his childhood home, while also seeing his own point of view approach and enter the front door. As he made his way through the house, images flashed before him—sudden glimpses of hands and feet being tied to a bed, of a bare man's chest and a woman's hands running over it. Something bad was happening, something wrong, but he couldn't quite figure out what it was.

Then he was standing outside the room, and it became momentarily clear. His father, wearing only his shorts, was the man tied to the bed, and straddling him was a woman who looked like his mother, but couldn't be his mother. She was slapping his father, saying horrible things to him. No woman would ever do that or say that to the man she loved. Would she?

And then suddenly, he was in the room, and the woman's head became separated from her body. It flew halfway across the room and landed with a *thump* on the carpeted floor, and even as it came to rest, the eyes seemed alive.

Her body, however, somehow stayed upright instead of falling. Blood gushed from the stump of her neck, a grotesque fountain splattering the walls and furniture, and raining down on his horrified father too, who screamed and screamed and screamed . . .

\*\*\*

George screamed too as he suddenly sat up in his bed, the last awful vestiges of the nightmare still playing before his eyes. The room was in almost total darkness, just a tiny bit of light streaming upward from the street and through the half-closed blinds.

His breathing slowed, gradually becoming normal. He was bathed in sweat, as he always was after one of the dreams. Fumbling in the darkness, he found the lamp on the bedside table, switched it on and yanked open the drawer. Coming up with a pill bottle, he managed to open it with his shaking hands and dropped a couple of pills into one palm, and then into his mouth.

Eventually, the bad feelings seeped from his mind, replaced by a sense of calm and control. It was almost like his mind was his again. But he knew that it wasn't. The drugs and the sessions with Dr. Williamson were helping, but they only went so far.

He knew he had to get out of here. Out of this city. He'd been here too long, and the change of scene hadn't helped. No matter what he and the doctors had done to try to purge him of the nightmares—and the urges—they were still there. Sometimes simmering, sometimes coming to a boil, but always there.

As he lay in the darkness, listening to the distant sounds of the city outside, it came to him where he needed to go. And why. And what he had to do before he left.

\*\*\*

# NIGHTMARE

George Tatum stared at Jackson from the four screens surrounding the central monitor in the computer room. It freaked Jackson out a little bit, and he had no idea why the system was set up like this; did he really need to see the guy's face gazing at him from all directions while he went over the man's case? He really needed to talk to someone about it, but for now there were more pressing matters. Tatum had his daily interview with Paul Williamson in a few minutes, and Jackson needed to get over there.

*Daily*, Jackson thought as he switched his cigar from one side of his mouth to the other, and glanced out the window at night, not day. It wasn't even 6, and the sun was already going down. Fucking winter. He hated it for a number of reasons, and one of them was going home in the dark after the workday, even if it ended on time at 5. Not that that had happened very much lately, with all the work the Tatum case had involved.

Still, there was an upside to that. The government money had been a boon to his practice, and among other things, it meant he'd been able to make Ellen and Clara very happy on Christmas morning. Of course, that had meant dealing with the crowds while doing the holiday shopping, which was another thing that annoyed him about this time of year, but . . .

He turned his attention back to the main monitor. Tatum's file information slowly scrolled up the screen:

**PATIENT: TATUM
CASE # 5306-8A
DIAGNOSIS:
SCHIZOPHRENIA
MILD AMNESIA
HOMICIDAL**

## MICHAEL GINGOLD

**DREAM FIXATION
SEIZURES**

And so on. He opened George's file and checked the most recent notations. All seemed to be going well. He closed the file and left the room, not bothering to turn off the computer. Tatum's face in quadruplicate watched him go.

A few minutes later, he was standing in the observation room with the rest of the team, watching through a one-way mirror as the red door in the room beyond opened, and George entered. He took out a cigarette and lit it, and after a couple of puffs he turned, facing Jackson and the others. The doctor standing closest to the light switch hurriedly snapped it off, plunging them into darkness, save what was leaking in from the other room.

Jackson shook his head a little. It wasn't like that would make any difference; George couldn't see past the mirror no matter how well lit up it was in here. Did he know someone was there, that he was being observed? Probably, if he watched enough TV. And given the suspicious look on George's face, he probably knew *something* was up.

Jackson stepped closer to the glass, trying to read George's expression. Was George just studying himself in the mirror, or trying to look past it, to determine whether he was alone or not?

He seemed just about ready to come closer when the red door opened again, and Dr. Paul Williamson entered. With his glasses and greying beard, he always struck Jackson as looking just like a generic shrink should look. He said something the group couldn't hear—the audio feed hadn't been turned on yet—then motioned for George to sit, and did the same.

## NIGHTMARE

From behind Jackson: "Has there been further progress?" It was the latest underling that Cooper, who was in charge of the government project, had sent to check in on how they were doing. Jackson didn't understand why Cooper seemed to send a new face down here every time he wanted an update; sometimes he amused himself with the thought that once each one submitted their report, they were killed so they couldn't reveal what they'd learned.

"There are still some psychotic episodes triggered by the dreams," Jackson answered. "Tatum's been Dr. Williamson's patient for a year now. We think the dreams are fixated on some childhood trauma, but Tatum can't or won't tell us. The experimental drugs are working for us. We can control the violent episodes, we just haven't succeeded in stopping the dreams. What we're trying to do now is modify them."

Dr. Williamson leaned in to begin talking to George, and Jackson turned to one of the tech guys. "Okay, Kurt, let's hear it," he said, snapping his fingers.

Kurt pushed a few buttons and turned a knob on the console beside him, and the sound from the next room came up. George was in the middle of talking as Dr. Williamson looked on sympathetically: " . . . two or three times now, always at the same moment. It's very strange."

"What else?" Dr. Williamson asked.

"It's like I . . . It's like I'm a child, there. I'm just a child."

"Now think, George. Are you looking at a child, or are you the child?"

George dropped his head into his hands for a moment, and came back up with a pained expression on his face. "Sometimes . . . I'm the child. Other times, it's like he's standing there. Then . . . again, I think I must be the child, but it . . . it can't be me. I'm really not . . . with a . . . "

"With a weapon, George?"

"It's not a weapon!" George raised his voice for the first time, then calmed again. "I can't tell. I can't see what it is. All I know is that something bad is just about to happen, or it starts to happen . . . and then they come in and they give me the pills, and it all disappears. Vanishes."

"You say something bad happens. Is it something you do, George?"

"I can't remember. It might be, but I just don't know. I know I don't want to do anything bad, and I sure don't want to see anything bad . . . but it happens anyway."

"So you have no control. Is that what scares you, George? The idea of losing control, of doing something you don't want to do?"

"Maybe. But sometimes it seems like . . . I'm just watching it. It's happening, and I want to look away but I can't. And I can never remember enough to know for sure."

"George, does anyone try to hurt you in your dreams? Do they do something to you that would make you want to hurt them back?"

George sat silently for a moment, as if searching his memory, before slowly shaking his head. "Not hurt me. Maybe someone else. It might be . . . someone I know getting hurt, and that's why it's so frightening."

"Is it someone you love, George? One of your parents, maybe?"

George shook his head. "I don't remember my parents. I can't even picture them, what they look like."

"Okay, all right." Dr. Williamson sat back. "It's been a good session, George. I think we learned a lot."

# NIGHTMARE

He got up, walked toward the mirror and, it seemed to Jackson, looked directly at him. Dr. Williamson knew someone was back here, all right.

"But I will want to talk to you about this again, George."

"So I can go, Dr. Williamson?"

"You can. You've got enough of the pills?"

"I do."

"Good. You let me know when you start running low."

George nodded, stood and left the room. Dr. Williamson watched him go, then looked back through the glass, arms folded.

Jackson looked over at Cooper's new stooge, who appeared to be satisfied. That was good. This project might have a happy ending after all.

\*\*\*

George turned off 6th Avenue and began walking down 42nd Street. He wasn't going back to the halfway house, not yet. He had managed to keep it together during the interview with Dr. Williamson, to present the side of himself that the doctor had wanted to see. But even as their talk had been coming to a close, he had felt the urges rising again. He needed to sate them, and knew where he needed to go to do it. Now that he was away, and outside, he already felt a little better.

He crossed the intersection of 7th Avenue and Broadway, dodged a cab that made a turn onto the street without even slowing down, and continued. Around him, the sounds of hookers and hustlers and the other street life, propositions being made, flesh and drugs being bought and sold. It was deafening, and he tried to ignore it, picking up his pace, looking up at the theater marquees as he approached and passed beneath them so he could avoid making eye contact with anyone. The titles were emblazoned in letters as big and loud as the noise of the street: THE MASTER AVENGERS. CALIGULA. FADE TO BLACK. SISTER STREET FIGHTER, FIVE DEADLY VENOMS and KUNG FU MASSACRE, those three all on one marquee.

And then, of course, there was the porn. The lurid titles and the suggestive images and the big X's and XXX's. Those movies might be enough to satisfy some people, but George needed more. And as he reached 8th Avenue, he spotted his destination and smiled.

Crossing the avenue, barely avoiding being hit by another cab whose driver apparently felt that red lights didn't apply to him, George reached the Show World Center and disappeared through the front door.

\*\*\*

## SCHIZOPHERNIA

Jackson looked down, blinked, then looked back up at the monitor, as if this action could somehow correct the mistake. No, it was still there.

## SCHIZOPHERNIA

How the hell did this happen? It had been spelled correctly only an hour ago. Had someone re-entered all the data for some stupid reason? What was the point? And if so, couldn't they have gotten that very common psychiatric term right?

He couldn't believe it. Or maybe he could. God knows the state of education was going downhill, with the schools trying to teach kids everything but basic reading and writing. He'd been stunned by some of the things Clara told him about her own high school. Now they were giving 15-year-olds sex education. Condoms

# NIGHTMARE

on bananas, for Christ's sake. No wonder no one could spell anymore.

Or maybe some joker around the office had done it as a gag. Well, *ha ha ha* if so. He glanced at the four Tatums regarding him from the secondary screens. Hell, maybe *he* had somehow done it. Stranger things had happened around here.

The rest of the data crept up the screen, Jackson watching it closely.

## MILD AMNESIA

Under the circumstances, he was surprised it didn't say MILK OF MAGNESIA.

## HOMICIDAL
## DREAM FIXATION
## SEIZURES

Alright, everything else there looked in order. He opened up Tatum's file and clicked on the little tape recorder sitting on the console.

"Karine, type this up first thing when you come in in the morning. See that it's distributed and put in Tatum's file, okay?"

He took the cigar out of his mouth and continued, "Case history synopsis: Tatum transferred from Braxton State Hospital for the Criminally Insane, remanded there by Fifth District Court after arrest as suspect in sexual mutilation and murder of Brooklyn family.

"Medical profile: intermittent epileptic seizures. Psychological profile: paranoid schizophrenia with delusions of grandeur and obsessive/compulsive dream ideation. The dream ideation apparently triggered violent psychotic attacks. Suffering from severe amnesia.

"Tatum's initial response to methacycladine was promising, later switched to our newest hypnotic drugs, hilamene and TL-54. He's shown rapid progress since, psychotic behavior has been extinguished, schizophrenia drug-controlled, seizures drug-controlled, obsessive-compulsive ideation is drug-controlled, and the dream fixations and the acting out have been modified by behavior techniques.

"Prognosis: Tatum is our first major success. We have taken a dangerous psychotic and completely rebuilt him. Programming him for future government or private sector use will be our next step. Um . . . my congratulations to one and all involved. Thanks, Karine."

He switched off the recorder and closed the file. On the main screen, the scroll came to its end:

**DREAM FIXATION:**
**DRUG CONTROLLED**
**PROBLEMS:**
**DREAMS HAVE TRIGGERED HOMICIDAL RAGE**
**TREATMENT PLAN:**
**PROGRAM TO SEE SELF RENDERED HELPLESS BY DRUG**
**RECOMMENDATION:**
**TATUM'S CURE IS MAJOR THERAPY BREAKTHROUGH IN BEHAVIOR CONTROL**
**INFORM MILITARY AND NATIONAL SECURITY DEPTS.**

Tomorrow was going to be a big day. Jackson smiled, replaced the cigar in his mouth and shut down the computer for the night. The four faces of Tatum flickered off to darkness.

***

The sliding door rose slowly with a mechanical *whirrrrrr*, revealing to George the large room behind it. From his little private booth, he could see the half dozen other men in similar booths ringing the space—but they were just in his peripheral vision, because his focus was on the girl. The gorgeous girl wearing nothing but a G-string and a pout. She danced in place to the tinny music on the weak speakers for a few moments, slowly turning, giving all her onlookers a good look at her perfect breasts.

George could barely keep his eyes off her gorgeous body, only glancing up at her face for the briefest moment. She was smiling, and for that quick glance it seemed she was smiling directly at him. Could she be thinking the same things about him that he was thinking about her? Did she want him to kiss her and touch her and make love to her? That was against the rules, but if she wanted it enough . . .

Now she was sashaying over to him, standing directly before him, shimmying her body as she looked down at him with that same smile. She had put herself within touching distance, and George knew she was giving him permission. She wanted his hands on her, caressing her full breasts as he kissed her sweet mouth, then pulling her to him as he undid his pants and—

He raised a hand slowly, reaching through the window toward the girl. She backed up a couple of steps, wagging a finger at him playfully, still smiling. George's face fell, but she didn't react to his disappointment, instead strutting across the room to another man in another window.

George fell back, watching her go, and—

## MICHAEL GINGOLD

*Suddenly flashed to his father, the woman on top of him, tying him down and slapping him—*

George shook the vision from his mind, refocusing on the girl. Perhaps if he made eye contact, he could persuade her to come back, to give him another chance.

Instead, the door slowly slid down with the same *whirrrrrr*, cutting her off from view.

Fine. It didn't matter. If she wouldn't give him her attention, there were other girls here who would.

He opened the red door and stepped out. The lower level of Show World was bustling with female workers and male customers and a few employees keeping an eye on everything. George scanned the room, sizing up the possibilities. At first a sexy blonde with a cigarette in her mouth seemed like she was responding to his gaze, but then she went into a booth, denying him.

The next girl who caught his eye didn't look away, though. She was a sultry-looking brunette wearing skimpy, sparkly lingerie, and makeup like bruises on her face. She licked her lips, and beckoned for George to follow her.

George entered the private booth and closed the door as the girl entered from the other side, a pane of glass stained with lipstick and cigarette burns and God knows what else between them. She picked up a phone receiver on her side, and he picked up the one next to him, noticing that while his had a metal-encased cord like a pay phone, hers was attached to a long spiral cord like the one he'd had—

*—at the apartment, where the visions and the urges had become too severe, to the point where he couldn't take it anymore, and he'd had to go upstairs and—*

# NIGHTMARE

"My name is Tara Alexander," came her voice over the line, snapping him out of it. "And what is your name, darling?"

"George," he said, his voice a halting quaver. She sat with her high-heeled shoes up on either side of the glass, giving him a good look at what was between her legs—and what wasn't. Her panties had somehow disappeared on her way into the booth.

She took out a vibrator, clicked it on and slipped it under her skirt, rubbing it delicately against her uncovered pussy. "Would you like to be doing this to me, George?" she purred, moaning softly. "Would you like to be touching me like this?"

Oh God, he would, and he wished he could reach right through the glass, or tear it down, and give her what she so obviously wanted.

"Ooooohhhhh, I wish it were you," she continued, closing her eyes and leaning her head back as she pleasured herself. "It's soooooo wonderful . . . "

He wanted that too, so badly, but he found he couldn't move, transfixed by the site of Tara getting herself off. He struggled to say something, but—

*—the woman (his mother?) slapped his father again, and again—*

"Just imagine the two of us together . . . " Tara sighed—

*—and now her head was gone, nothing left but the stump that fountained blood into the air—*

"Oh, George, I know it could be like this!"

*The blood continued to gush from the ravaged neck like it would never stop, splattering down onto the bed and the walls and—*

"Oh, why aren't you in here with me?!" Tara cried as she brought herself to a climax, gasping and sighing, her head thrown back, eyes squeezed shut in ecstasy . . .

## MICHAEL GINGOLD

Not seeing that George had collapsed to the floor, twitching and shuddering, his own eyes closed tight, but in misery instead of pleasure, spittle foaming in the corners of his mouth. Mercifully, a partition came down between them, blocking him from her sight, before she was finished and could take in the sight of him.

*And he saw himself standing before the decapitated body and his bound father, a bloody axe in his hand, and he suddenly became aware of what he had to do next . . .*

George's eyes snapped open. This was the part that he had never told Dr. Williamson, that he did, in fact, clearly see the weapon in his hand at the end of the nightmares or visions or whatever they were, and that as terrified as that made him, it also gave him a sense of purpose. One that he knew just how to fulfill.

And he knew just how to fulfill it now.

\*\*\*

Lindsey Parker cringed at what was happening up on the screen, and not for the first time. As she watched, a madman cut into a dead woman's forehead and sliced across, blood streaming from the slit, and then grabbed onto her scalp and roughly yanked it off her head, the camera never shying away.

There were a few whoops and hollers from the people seated around them—none of them sitting too close, thank God, though it still made her nervous. She looked at Jeremy, and to his credit he had a look of revulsion on his face. But if he was grossed out as she was, why were they still sitting there watching this? She liked a good scary movie as much as anybody, but this one was too much.

They'd seen and enjoyed a few horror films before; in fact, their first date had been to see *The Shining* the

## NIGHTMARE

night before Halloween. As a freshman film student, Jeremy was anxious to introduce her to the genius of Stanley Kubrick, and she agreed it was pretty great (though she preferred *Dr. Strangelove* when they saw it at a revival house a month or so later).

Lindsey had always enjoyed going to the movies, but once she and Jeremy started dating, she gained a new appreciation of them. His passion for cinema started rubbing off on her, in part because she hadn't known anyone before who was as focused on their future as she was. Most of her high school friends had only possessed vague ideas of what they wanted to do with their lives after graduation, but Lindsey had become determined at the age of 14 to become a teacher, and pursued it with single-minded dedication. Her and Jeremy's fields of study were very different, yet they had sparked to each other's commitment to their goals.

She had sparked with Jeremy on a physical level, too. Behind his glasses and shaggy hair, he was one good-looking guy, and he made her feel beautiful too. The blazing, copper-colored hair that made her the object of teasing when she was growing up was, he often said, one of his favorite things about her. When the holiday season had rolled around, he had taken to calling her "my Christmas girl" because of her red hair and green eyes, and she swooned a little bit inside every time he said it.

They also shared a sense of adventure, and often spent their weekends poking around odd corners of the city. It had been his idea to check out a movie at one of the 42nd Street theaters instead of the classier venues they usually attended, and to find the most "gross and cheesy" movie they could. Well, this one was gross, all right, but it wasn't cheesy in a fun way, not like the schlocky B-flicks they sometimes watched together on late-night TV.

She really wanted to leave, but after the scalping scene passed and she glanced at Jeremy again, he seemed pretty caught up in it. So she figured she'd sit through the rest of the movie with him, and afterward they could go get coffee somewhere and joke about how disgusting it was, and this was one adventure they could check off the list and not have to experience ever again. Lindsey even smiled as she thought that to make up for it, she could insist he take her to see a nice movie like *Popeye*—one he was dead set against, unable to comprehend how a great artist like Robert Altman could make a movie based on a comic strip, starring a guy from a sitcom.

But first, she had to pee. She'd been holding it in for a little while, hoping she could hold out till the movie was over, but now she realized that wasn't going to happen. She leaned over and whispered, "There's a bathroom here, right?"

"Yeah," he whispered back. "I think it's downstairs."

"Okay. I'll be right back."

"All right. Just . . . " He stopped.

"Just what?"

"Be quick," he said after a moment. "You don't want to miss any of this."

He grinned as he said it, and she gave him a little swat on the arm before making her way down the row of dingy, tattered seats. He had acknowledged she wasn't having the greatest time, and she appreciated that. She also thought that what he initially intended to say was "Be careful," but then he didn't want to scare her, and she appreciated that too.

She reached the aisle and headed up to the rear of

## NIGHTMARE

the theater, her shoes squishing in the carpet as she walked. This whole place was gross, in fact, and the other patrons didn't seem much better. She tried to catch out of the corner of her eye whether any of them were watching her as she proceeded, but it was hard to see in the dark. As she approached the rear doors, she almost tripped over the cat she'd noticed prowling around the auditorium when they first arrived. She had tried not to think about what it was doing there.

In the lobby, she found the signs for the restrooms, which were indeed on the lower level. Trying not to look anxious, she made her way down the stairs and into the ladies' room. There was no door, just an opening, and as soon as she stepped in she was greeted by a smell that almost drove her right back out, and made her half consider trying her luck in the men's room. But she could just imagine how one of this theater's male customers might react upon discovering a woman there, so she resolved to breathe through her mouth, and went to the stall furthest from the doorway.

What she saw when she opened the door made her close it right back again. *Oh, shit*, she thought, then giggled at her extremely appropriate reaction. Opening the next stall over, she was relieved to find it clean—at least comparatively—closed the door, and was about to drop her jeans when she noticed there was no latch on the door.

"Oh, shit." This time out loud. The door was too far from the toilet for her to hold it closed while she did her business, so she tried the last stall, praying the third time would be the charm. And it was. Clean—again, relatively—with a latch, and she noticed it was the only one with a full roll of TP. Tearing off a long strip, she cleaned the seat as best she could, and sat down. She peed quickly, hit the flush handle—and nothing happened.

It occurred to her that leaving the toilet unflushed wouldn't make the slightest difference in a place like this, but she decided to give it just one more try for decorum's sake. She pushed the handle down, held it, and after a couple of seconds it flushed successfully. She turned to leave, and that's when she heard the footsteps.

Something about them immediately put Lindsey on edge. They didn't sound like the casual steps of someone coming in to relieve themselves, but were a little slower, more deliberate. She quietly retreated back and sat down on the toilet, leaning down to peer under the stall door.

The legs and feet clad in men's pants and shoes crossed the room and stopped in front of the stalls. She thought for a moment that maybe he had come in from the men's room, where it might be even fouler than it was in here. Now he was wondering if the stalls were empty, and it was safe to use one of them. Perhaps she should extend her feet in front of her, so he could see this one was occupied and didn't—

Then the figure stepped closer, and suddenly the stall door was hit hard from outside. "Hey!" she yelled, hoping that alerting whoever it was to her presence would make him stop. Instead, the door was banged again, and again, more aggressively each time.

"Stop that! Go away! Go away!" she screamed as the door continued to shake. She frantically looked around, and down, and realized she could slip under the side of the stall and probably make it out of the room before—

*Snap!* The latch came apart in two pieces that clattered to the tile floor. The door swung in violently, and behind it, the man glared in at Lindsey. For a

# NIGHTMARE

moment, she felt a sense of something like relief. This guy didn't look like the creep she'd expected to see, one with greasy hair and a contorted face and maybe a scar or two. With his glasses and mild features, he looked almost like an accountant, or even one of her professors at school.

Then she looked into his eyes, and an awful chill washed over her. She had heard people describe a few times how they had seen another person's eyes and known immediately that they were crazy, and that's the feeling she had now. The man's gaze was cold, devoid of human feeling, like there was something else behind them, something that had long ago taken leave of any sense of sanity.

*Oh God oh God*, her mind raced, *oh God please please let me get out of here let me get back to where it's safe and back to Jeremy and I promise I'll never ever ever go to a horrible disgusting place like this again I promise I promise oh please God just let me get out . . .*

But all that escaped her lips was a helpless "No . . ." before his hands closed around her throat.

***

Jeremy couldn't wait any longer. It hadn't been very long since Lindsey had left, but they'd been dating long enough for him to know by now that it didn't take her this long to go to the bathroom. Especially on those rare occasions when she had to go during a movie; usually she'd be back in a flash, hurrying to her seat and whispering to him, "What did I miss?" The first time, she returned so fast that he whispered back jokingly, "Did you wash your hands?" and she responded "Yes" while putting her hands all over his face. Her mischievous sense of humor was one of the many things he loved about her.

## MICHAEL GINGOLD

Now he was getting concerned. He knew theaters like this could be pretty rough, which was why he'd suggested they go to a weekday show, when there would be fewer people here. He had even asked a friend familiar with these places if there would be serious danger involved, and had been reassured that as rowdy as the audiences could get, actual risk of attack or assault was pretty low. And when Lindsey went for the restroom, he had turned in his seat, trying not to be too obvious about it, and watched to be sure no one else got up and followed her out.

Maybe she'd had trouble finding a clean stall. It could be that she hadn't, and had run out to one of the other places on 42nd or even up to the HoJo's at 46th to find a bathroom there. Even though, unlike himself, she hadn't grown up in the city, she'd learned quickly how to look after herself on its streets.

Or it could be that once she'd left the auditorium, she decided she just didn't want to see any more of the movie, and was waiting in the lobby for it to finish and for him to come out. That wasn't like her, to leave him hanging like that, but it was a reasonable explanation, because nothing bad could have happened to her . . .

But now he had to check. And if it turned out that she was in the lobby, he would leave right away with her. They'd experienced enough of what one of these theaters was like, and even half a movie's worth was enough.

The lobby was empty when he came out; even the ticket taker had evidently taken a break. Jeremy went to the front doors, opened one and looked around outside, quickly determining that Lindsey wasn't there. Okay, so he would definitely wait here for her. Whether she had gone to the bathrooms downstairs or left to find one, she had to come back through here.

# NIGHTMARE

Except that he had the nagging feeling he should go down to the restrooms right now and check for her there. Just to be sure.

The lower level was as deserted as the upper when he got to the bottom of the stairs. Feeling a little embarrassed even though there was no reason to be, he called out, "Lindsey?"

No response. He stepped closer to the entrance to the ladies' room, and was about to call out again.

Then his eyes slipped down to the floor beneath the nearest stall, and suddenly he couldn't speak. He couldn't even move for a few moments, before he was dreadfully compelled to enter the room and approach the stall.

The shoes visible in front of the toilet weren't recognizable as Lindsey's; they wouldn't be recognizable as anyone's, they were so drenched in dark red. Yet as Jeremy slowly came around to the front of the stall, the door was ajar enough that he didn't have to open it any further to see inside, and then he knew. Yet he couldn't bring himself at first to look up past her legs, her jeans also streaked with blood. Or her stomach, which had been savaged to the point that a nub of intestine hung out, lying flaccid across her lap.

His mind desperately tried to deny what he was seeing, that the destroyed body before him had been his sweet, perfect girlfriend only a few minutes ago—before he had decided they should come to this foul place. And yet, he needed to confirm that it was her, that it wasn't by some ridiculous chance someone else who just happened to be dressed like Lindsey, and he forced his eyes higher, to her face.

And the moment he saw her wide, staring eyes, he knew that the look in those eyes would haunt him forever, because he knew that the plea behind them was *Jeremy, where are you??*

He tore himself away from the sight, and made it to a sink on the other side of the room just in time to heave his guts all over the porcelain.

# THE SECOND DAY

**G**EORGE STOOD ON the deck of the Staten Island Ferry, watching the twin towers of the World Trade Center and the other downtown buildings recede into the distance. He felt an unusual sense of calm watching Manhattan drift into the distance; such a big city, and yet it looked so small from here. He had come to feel lost while in the midst of it—too much of what Dr. Williamson called external stimuli—and now he was putting it behind him, in his past, as he set out to achieve his new purpose.

The cold wind off the water had driven most of the other passengers inside, but not George. He found it refreshing, and turned to face forward, watching as the Statue of Liberty slowly slid by to the right of the boat. It would be the last time he saw these landmarks, he thought, and the last time he would experience weather like this. It was a lot warmer where he was going.

Once the ferry docked, George made his way quickly out of the Staten Island terminal and found a pay phone. As he fished in the pocket of his trenchcoat for a dime, he had a sudden flash of concern—did he remember the number? But of course he did. He couldn't forget it, even all these years later.

He dropped the dime in the slot, and dialed the number.

## MICHAEL GINGOLD

\*\*\*

The ringing phone almost drew Susan out from under the covers. It wouldn't have taken much effort to reach out from the bed and answer it, but she didn't even feel like doing that. The stress of last night's drama had drained her, and she preferred to just lie there in the semidarkness of her bedroom till a little before 11, when she would be heading out to see Bob. Besides, one of the kids could pick it up downstairs, and sure enough, the third ring was the last one and she vaguely heard C.J. say, "Hello?"

The boy stood by the downstairs extension, holding the receiver tight to his ear as Tammy and Kim bustled around him, getting ready for school. He didn't hear a response, so he stepped into the next room, the long cord allowing him to get a little further from the noise.

"Hello?" he repeated. Again, no answer, though now he could hear faint noises in the background, like water and boats, and the distant screech of a seagull. "Bob?" If it was Bob, he didn't say anything, which didn't make any sense. Bob was the only one who seemed to like to talk to C.J. these days.

"Who is this?" C.J. asked, and the reply was a *click* and the line went dead. He shrugged; if that was a prank call, it wasn't much of a prank. It wasn't at all as funny as the ones he would make sometimes, like calling the butcher shop and asking if they had pig's feet, and when the reply was yes, saying, "Where do you buy your shoes?"

He replaced the receiver in its cradle, and was about to get his own school stuff ready when Susan yelled down from upstairs.

"C.J., who was that on the phone?" Still deep in her bed, she hoped it wasn't Bob changing their plans;

# NIGHTMARE

she really needed quality time with him today. "I don't know, they didn't answer!" she heard C.J. shout back. Okay, it wasn't Bob—that was all that really mattered right now. She reached over to the bedside lamp, clicked it on, and noticed the time on the clock beside it.

"You all better hurry, or you're going to miss your bus!"

"Okay!" That was Tammy, and since she was the most comparatively disciplined of the three, Susan trusted that she could get them all to the bus stop in Susan's absence. Sure enough, after a few more sounds of activity from downstairs, she heard, "Bye!" "See you later, Mom!" Then the sound of the front door opening and closing, and, through the window, their footsteps on the front path as they headed down to the bus stop.

At last, she was alone. She relished these days off, the one day a week when she didn't have to leave at the same time as the kids to get to work at the store, when she could sleep in or just lounge in bed, enjoying the silence.

She couldn't really do that this morning, though. The thing with C.J. last night still had her a little on edge. She had spoken to him about it, and he had denied he had done anything wrong, which only made her more angry. If he could just admit to his misbehavior, they could talk about why he had done it, and maybe get to the root of the strange way he'd been acting. Instead, she had just become frustrated, and spoken to him more harshly. She regretted it the moment she had gone to bed last night, and thought that maybe she would try talking to him again this morning.

Instead, she had woken up to the sounds of the kids running around downstairs, and decided she needed to have that discussion when it was the two of them alone, not with Tammy and Kim looking on. Besides, she could talk it over with Bob today; his was always a sympathetic ear, and his advice was sound much more often than not.

She got out of bed, and went to the bathroom to take a shower. Under the hot water, she felt the tension ease away. It would be a better day today, she was sure of it.

\*\*\*

Dr. Williamson sat at his desk, working up the resolve to push the button on his phone. He knew what the answer would be, knew what the ramifications were. But maybe if he waited just a little longer, the news at the other end of the line would be good news, and their concerns would be for naught.

He turned in his chair and looked out the window. From up here on the 28th floor, he had a terrific view of midtown, and Central Park just a few blocks away. It was a beautiful, sunny, crisp but not too cold day, and he could just imagine all the people out there enjoying it, taking walks in the park, maybe skating at Wollman Rink. At this moment, he wished he were one of them—anyone but himself right now.

It was going to be bad news, he decided, no matter how much longer he waited. He let out a resigned breath and punched the button.

"Kathleen, has George Tatum arrived yet?"

"No, I'm afraid not, Doctor," said the woman's voice over the speaker. "Have you checked where he's staying?"

"I did. Twice. They haven't seen him either."

"Okay. I'll keep an eye out for him, let you know if he shows up."

"Thank you, Kathleen." He pushed the button

# NIGHTMARE

again. Yep, still bad news. He wondered how long it would take Jackson to find out. Or maybe Jackson already knew, and was on his way over to give him what Dr. Williamson was sure would be a very large piece of his mind.

Dr. Williamson tried to push down the sense of helplessness rising within him. He couldn't call the police about this; there would be all kinds of questions about the way they'd handled Tatum, which would inevitably lead to revelations about the program, and who was backing it. Perhaps they could get a good PI involved, someone who could track Tatum down while attracting a minimum of attention. Dr. Williamson didn't know of any himself, but he knew Jackson did. So he would ask Jackson once he was aware of what was going on.

Or maybe the afternoon would bring a miracle, and word that Tatum had not in fact disappeared from all the places he was supposed to be, and was not roaming the streets of New York or, more likely, getting out of the city as quickly and quietly as possible. As Dr. Williamson stood and looked out the window, wishing again he could be any one of the carefree people strolling in Central Park, he felt there had to be a simple explanation.

He just couldn't think of one right now.

\*\*\*

George drove his Ford Maverick out of the gas station and onto the two-lane road that would take him back to I-95. He was making good time, and if he kept up this pace he would make it to his destination before sunrise the next morning.

As he pulled onto the main highway and took his place in the flow of traffic, he checked the rearview mirror. It was an involuntary action; there wasn't going to be anyone following him. By this point, no doubt people would have started noticing he wasn't turning up where he was supposed to, but how long would it take them to start seriously looking? After all, it had been 10 days since he'd quit that job they'd found for him, and neither Dr. Williamson nor anyone else had brought it up. Those doctors weren't as smart as they seemed to—

The thought was interrupted by a rattling from the engine. George frowned and looked down at the dashboard. Everything seemed okay there, and after another couple of bangs and clanks, the engine settled back into a smooth thrumming sound.

Perhaps he shouldn't have let the Maverick sit for so long, he thought, or maybe he should have put it in a garage instead of that outdoor lot at the Staten Island waterfront. But then, he quickly corrected himself, there would have been a record that the car had been there, and the whole idea was to keep it somewhere it wouldn't be noticed. That way, if someone tried to follow him from the apartment, he could easily lose them in the turmoil of the subways instead of getting into the car there. Then a quick hop onto the Staten Island Ferry and into the car, and he'd be gone if need be. He'd made sure to sneak out there every couple of months or so since he'd started the program with Dr. Williamson, and give the car a little run around the local roads just to keep the battery charged. But sitting out there for so long, exposed to the elements and whatever else, who knows what problems the engine might have?

Well, there was nothing he could do about it now. And it just had to keep going for less than a day. Once he got down there, any problems could be dealt with. Everything was going to be fine.

# NIGHTMARE

\*\*\*

Bob Rosen looked up from the deck of his sailboat, and smiled as he saw Susan running across the street from the parking lot and toward the marina. Even from here, he could tell she was smiling too, and that pleased him. She'd been in quite a state when he'd left her last night, and he was hoping a good night's sleep, and maybe a long talk with C.J., would make things better. And it appeared they had, as she ran up the gangway and onto the pier, and it seemed to him her smile got bigger.

"How ya doin'?" he said with a wave as she approached the boat. He decided he wasn't going to ask about last night's goings-on. If she brought them up, he would let her vent, but no need to remind her if she had already put them out of her mind.

"Let's go, babe!" he continued. "Time and tide wait for no man!" She laughed, and then they were embracing, her arms around his shirtless body and him holding her just as tight as they kissed. It lingered a little longer than usual, and Bob thought for a moment that they should just head below decks right now, and not even bother launching. He didn't want to appear too eager, though, until he had a read on where her mind was at.

So when they separated, he just said, "You look great. You want to be captain today?"

"Sure!" she replied.

Instead, once they had set out onto Indian River, and passed under the Causeway bridge, it was Bob at the wheel as usual. Not that he minded; he was perfectly happy to steer them while Susan lay in the cockpit, her eyes closed, enjoying the solitude of the open water. It was an escape for her, one he knew she valued, just as he did. There was a feeling of freedom out here, from work and kids and all the other responsibilities, that just made him want to—well, sing.

"Fifteen men on a dead man's chest, yo ho ho and a bottle of rum!" She smiled again, and he continued, "Drink and the devil have done with the rest, yo ho ho and a bottle of rummmmmm."

"Have you got any?" she asked.

"Any what?"

"Rum. I could use a little right now."

Uh-oh. So she was still a little troubled, it seemed. "Sorry, hon. I can pick some up tonight. Or maybe we'll come across a ship we can plunder," he said, with the gravelly voice of a buccaneer.

"All by ourselves?"

"We can take 'em," he said, continuing the act. "There ain't a crew alive I couldn't defeat!" Then back to his normal tone: "You know, sometimes I think in another life, I really must have been a pirate."

"Well, you have the black beard," she laughed.

"And I drive a Cutlass."

"That's right. All you need now is an eyepatch and a parrot."

"Nah. I prefer to keep both my eyes. And parrots are a pain. All they do is squawk in your ear and poop on your shoulder."

She laughed again, and then there was silence. The comfortable silence of two people completely at ease with each other. Nonetheless, Bob felt she was holding something back, and wondered if he should venture to ask what was troubling her. Before he had to make a decision, she said, "Sounds like the kids. The squawking part, not the pooping."

Okay, here goes. "Everyone better today?"

"I guess so. I didn't really talk to C.J. this morning, but last night he was denying what he did."

# NIGHTMARE

"What did he do?"

"As far as I can tell, he put on a scary mask and went outside and looked in the windows, and scared Kathy and the girls."

"He looked in on the girls? On the second floor?"

"I'm pretty sure, yes. He must have been up on the roof. I've told him a hundred times not to climb up there, but he just won't listen."

"Were you able to get Kathy settled down?"

"Eventually. I just hoped he hasn't frightened her away for good."

"He's acting out. A lot of kids do at his age. He just needs to grow out of it."

"I don't know if I can wait that long. Tammy and Kim never behaved like this."

"Little boys are different."

"Were you like that when you were his age?"

"You mean scaring people? No. But I made my parents crazy other ways. We had a little sailboat back then, smaller than this one, and sometimes in the summer I would just get up in the morning, jump in that boat and head out on the water without telling them. When I'd get back, they'd be freaking out. I lost a lot of allowances doing that."

"Well, I feel sorry for your parents. I can understand what they went through."

"Yeah, but I turned out okay in the end, didn't I?"

"You did." She smiled again. That was good. She stood, and gave him a little kiss on the lips. "You turned out great."

They kissed again, and he said, "I'll have a talk with C.J. Man to man. See if I can't set him straight."

"I appreciate that. I really do." They kissed again, longer this time, and lay down on the padded bench of the cockpit. She gripped him tighter, her fingernails digging into his bare back—a sensation that he loved, and she knew it. He slipped a hand up under the back of her blouse, reaching her bra, undoing it with one deft flick of his fingers. The move always came easy to him, ever since he was a teenager, and he often wondered back then why so many guys acted like it was some impossible physical task, akin to undoing the Gordian Knot.

Her breath came sharper and faster as he slid his hand around to her breasts, caressing them and running his fingertips back and forth across her nipples. They perked up right away, and he resisted the urge to just tear her blouse open, sending buttons flying every which way. Instead, he began slowly undoing them, from the top down, his eyes never leaving hers, the anticipation in both their eyes making the moment even more exciting.

Then her blouse was open and her bra was up by her neck and he was kissing her breasts, his tongue teasing her nipples as her breath came in long, passionate sighs. He looked up briefly and saw her eyelids open, her eyes rolled back, showing only white. It was a sight that might have spooked some guys, but to Bob it was insanely exciting—she was completely lost in the arousal, as was he.

He kissed and licked his way down her stomach, relishing the softness of her skin to his lips and tongue, her sighs becoming louder as he reached her jeans. He undid the top button with his teeth—another trick he had mastered at a tender age—and slowly drew the zipper down. She arched her body to make it easier for him to slide her jeans and her panties off at the same time, and in seconds they were free of her and he was kissing her inner thighs, slowly working his way up and just stopping short, teasing her until—

# NIGHTMARE

Susan gasped as she felt his tongue inside her, spreading her legs and grabbing his hair like she wanted to tear it out. He found her sweet spot and she moaned louder, louder, encouraging him to lick faster and faster until she screamed, writhing beneath him, her legs rising and wrapping around him. He kept up the licking, loving her warmth and her wetness and her ecstasy, until her cries subsided. Her body relaxed and she let go of his hair, her arms falling limply to her sides.

He let her come down for a little while before he began kissing and licking his way back up her body, to her neck and her ears and then his lips found hers, gentler this time. When they separated, she opened her eyes and whispered, "That was wonderful."

"What do you mean, 'was'?" he asked.

"Hmm?"

"I'm not done with you yet," he said, a mischievous smile spreading across his face. He reached down and began undoing his own jeans, and she smiled sweetly back at him.

## THE SECOND NIGHT

**T**HE SUN WAS just beginning to go down when the engine began knocking and sputtering again. This time, it didn't go away after a few seconds, and George frowned. If this had to happen, couldn't it have happened during the day, when there was a better chance he could find a repair shop?

When he had crossed the border into South Carolina, he figured he was home free. The trip was more than halfway done, just two more states to go, and the songs he was picking up on the local radio station were helping keep his mind occupied. Just a few minutes earlier, the DJ had been plugging "the Seaside Holiday Inn Lounges at downtown North Myrtle Beach and Surfside, home of the famous Myrtle Monster, the tallest, meanest, wildest drink in captivity! And while you sip a Monster or two, you can get into the best music on the beach."

*Sipping a Monster*, he thought. *They don't know what a monster is.* He wondered if anybody at the Seaside Holiday Inn Lounges had ever really encountered something so frightening that they—

Then his dark reverie was interrupted by the misfiring engine. He slowed his speed, hoping that he'd just been straining it by going too fast, but the noises continued. Now there was nothing to do but pull

# NIGHTMARE

over, and that thought caused him more concern. If he stopped at the side of I-95, it wouldn't be long before the cops found the car. No doubt his absence had been noticed by now, and he certainly didn't want anyone figuring out what direction he was headed.

His frustration was building to the breaking point when good fortune beckoned in the form of an exit sign. It was for a local road, just a half mile down the highway. If the car could just hold together long enough to get off that exit, and far enough down . . .

After 40 seconds that seemed to drag on for eternity, he swerved off down the exit lane, emerging onto a narrow, winding road with only the occasional streetlamp. Snapping on the high beams, he squinted into the half-lit darkness ahead of him, seeking a good place to turn off as the commotion from the engine got louder.

Finally, he spotted a dirt road and instinctively steered down it, into even deeper darkness. There was nothing visible in the edges of the headlights but trees and rocks, and George couldn't see any visible tire tracks ahead of him. It was like no one had traveled down this path in a long time, and that's just what he wanted.

A couple of lights became visible in the distance, and George lifted his gaze off the road to focus on them, and then suddenly the road ran out in front of him and he braked hard, bringing the car sliding to a stop. With one last rattle, the engine died, and the dashboard lights went out. It was done.

George opened the glove compartment and rifled through the limited contents, pushing aside folded maps and other paper detritus until he found a flashlight. Clicking it on, he found the hood latch and flipped it, a metallic *clunk* answering him from outside. He got out, lifted the hood, inspected the engine. Other than the smoke or steam wafting from one of the components, he couldn't identify the problem, and it wasn't like he knew how to fix it anyway, nor did he have any tools other than the jack and spare in the trunk.

He slammed the hood down, then banged on it with his fist. Now that he'd gotten the car far enough off the road to avoid immediate detection, he had his own situation to deal with. He was in Middle of Nowhere, SC, somewhere in the Myrtle Beach area, though he had no idea how far that was, and he needed another car.

He looked back up at the distant lights and trained the flashlight in front of him. What he saw was water, gently lapping against a strip of sand too tiny to be called a beach. Those lights were on the other side of what appeared to be a pretty expansive lake. It would be far to walk, but George had no other choice. And maybe he'd run into something or someone else on the way.

Hoping the batteries in the flashlight would hold out, he headed back down the dirt road.

\*\*\*

Barbara Stockton pulled her Oldsmobile into Gatsby's parking lot, circling the other cars till she found a spot on the far side. It was busy tonight, she thought as she brought the car to a stop, and that gave her a sense of relief. It wasn't likely that Steve would make a scene, but it was even less so if they were in a crowded place.

She checked herself in the rearview mirror, tilting her head a little to catch the illumination from one of the lights surrounding the lot. Then she chuckled to herself; she wasn't out to impress anyone with her looks tonight, but old habits die hard. Besides, she

# NIGHTMARE

possessed what her mother and her friends and even Steve had called "natural beauty," and with her big brown eyes and lush dark hair, she figured maybe they were right. Whatever she had, she hoped she could keep it once she turned 30 in a few years, and awhile after that.

Barbara got out of the car and walked quickly to Gatsby's front entrance, disappearing inside. For a few seconds, all was still. Then George emerged from the wooded darkness beyond the parking lot. He started for Barbara's car, then stopped and looked in the direction she had gone. Changing course, he headed for the entrance.

Inside, the place was indeed packed, with the din of conversation and silverware clanking on porcelain in the restaurant area competing with the voices and music in the bar. Tonight's performer strummed his guitar and sang, "Gonna take some time, till I get myself together again . . . " Barbara thought that sounded appropriate as she sought Steve out, and found him sitting at one end of the bar, an open stool beside him.

He was still in his shirtsleeves and tie, and flashed her a big grin when he saw her approaching. She always found that grin goofy yet endearing; it was one of the things that had first attracted her to him when they began working at the firm together. She'd felt at ease with him right from the start, and it was easy to say yes the first time he asked her out. And things had gone well, for the most part; it was just that—

"Hi, honey," he said as he stood to greet her, leaning in for a kiss. She turned her head just slightly so that he kissed her cheek, and she kissed his. When he stepped back, she hoped not to see disappointment in his eyes, and was relieved that she didn't. Instead, that smile again.

"Have a seat," he said, and that was one of the things she didn't find so endearing. Of course she was going to have a seat, and he had a habit of telling her—not forcefully, just casually—to do things it was obvious she was going to do, or had to do. It bothered her more at work, where it felt like Steve asserting his superior position on the Bleichman and Fitz totem pole, especially when he did it in front of their co-workers. She didn't think he ever actually meant to put her down; it was just his manner of speaking. But it still got to her.

"How's your cousin?" he asked, and that Barbara did appreciate. She had told him she needed to stop at home instead of going straight to Gatsby's after work, to call her parents and find out how Megan, who had suffered a stroke that startled everyone due to her young age, was doing. "She's getting better," Barbara replied. "They said she might be out of the hospital by next week."

"Well, that's good news. Let's drink to that!" He managed to catch the bartender's eye, and as the man approached, told Barbara, "I know what you're having."

There it was again. Barbara knew he was just trying to be nice, to demonstrate a familiarity and be a gentleman by ordering for her. Not meaning anything by it.

"Double bourbon and a gin and tonic, please." While he ordered, she took a quick scan of the bar. She told herself she wasn't looking to see if anyone they knew, especially from the firm, was there, though she felt a quick rush of relief that no one was. Just a lot of couples and groups of friends, all seeming to have a good time. Except one guy about halfway down, sitting by himself, not paying much attention to the drink in

# NIGHTMARE

front of him. With his trenchcoat and glasses, he seemed to Barbara like he might be a private detective of some kind—and since he was here by himself in a popular watering hole, maybe he was.

He looked around, his eyes meeting hers for just a second before jumping away. He wasn't investigating her, at any rate, Barbara thought.

"To Megan," Steve said, and she turned her attention back to him. He was holding their drinks, which had come quickly considering the crowd. She took hers, clinked glasses with him, and they both took a sip.

"That's some good news," he said. "I guess we could both use it, the way the Lieber case is going . . . "

"Remember, Steve, no-work zone," she said, gesturing to the bar around them.

"Right, sorry." He took another drink. "So what are we talking about, then?"

She saw no reason to avoid or delay the subject. "Steve, I think we need to slow things down a little."

"Between us?" She nodded. "Why, what's wrong?"

"Nothing's wrong. And I just want to say, before anything else, this has nothing to do with anything you've done. If anything, I think I might have rushed into this a little too fast."

"Barbara, if it felt like I was rushing you, I'm sorry, that wasn't my intent." She believed him; he'd been eager, of course, but he hadn't forced her into anything, and had listened when she'd said there were certain things she wasn't comfortable with.

"I know it wasn't, Steve. But I've taken a step back and looked at how things are going, and I'm just thinking . . . " She stopped, trying to decide how to put what she was feeling into words. It wasn't coming, and all she knew was what she *didn't* want to tell him, especially given the look in his eyes. "I'm not going to say let's just be friends, because I do want more than that. I just feel like . . . we skipped the part where we really get to know each other."

He smiled. "We've gotten to know each other pretty well. It's been two months since we first went out to . . . "

"I know it has. But the last time, at your place . . . afterwards it just felt like a step I wasn't ready to take." She could tell he didn't quite get what she was saying, but the more articulate nature that served her so well at the firm was eluding her now. "Look, what I simply want to say is that I want to keep seeing you. Let's just . . . put the brakes on things a little, okay?"

He sat silently for a moment, then finished his double bourbon in one drink. He seemed hurt, and she was trying to think of a less clichéd way to say *It's not you, it's me*, but nothing was occurring to her.

"So you don't want this to be physical," he finally answered. There it was, just the facts.

"That's not what I'm saying. I just want to give that part a little more time, that's all."

He considered that for a moment, then put his glass back on the bar, a little more forcefully than she was comfortable with. *Here we go*, she thought. *Here's where it either becomes a scene or it doesn't.*

Fortunately, it didn't. No accusations flew, no voice was raised. Instead, he seemed resigned. "Then I guess we'll see how it goes," he said. "I really do care about you."

"I know you do. Thank you for understanding."

"You'll find I'm a very understanding guy," he said, flashing that smile again, and then raising his hand to signal the bartender. Barbara glanced around at the other patrons, thankful that they hadn't had to

## NIGHTMARE

witness anything turning ugly. She didn't notice that the guy who looked like he might be a private detective was gone.

The next hour or so passed pleasantly, and things relaxed between them, and Barbara felt she really did want to keep things going with Steve, and take things to the next level once she was fully comfortable with that. As he settled their tab, he asked if she wanted to come over to his place for a little while, just for a nightcap, but she said no, she was feeling tired and wanted to head home, and he accepted that with good grace.

As they stepped out of Gatsby's, he went in for another kiss, and this time she let it reach her lips, just for a few seconds. "Goodnight," he said, and she replied in kind and started across the parking lot. She was halfway to the car when she sensed him behind her, and turned.

"Barbara . . . " he began, and she felt it best not to let him continue. "Please understand, not tonight, okay?" she said, trying to be firm but not unkind.

"Okay. Drive safe. I'll call you soon, make sure you get home all right."

It wasn't necessary, but she did appreciate his concern. "Don't worry about me, I'm going right home. Good night."

She went to her car and got in, fighting a sense of disappointment. They had left things off in a good spot, and then he had to put a damper on it by going for one last attempt at getting her back to his place. As she put the engine in gear and drove out of the lot onto the road, she wondered if that was a sign of things to come, whether he really would accept her need to slow their course. It was all she could think about as she headed home.

## MICHAEL GINGOLD

She certainly never thought to look in the dark space in front of the car's back seat.

\*\*\*

When Barbara got home, she tossed her keys on top of the TV set, dropped her purse on the couch, slipped off her jacket and let it fall to the floor. She had just moved into the house a year ago, and while she generally tried to keep it neat and tidy, it was her first time having her own place, and she enjoyed the license that gave her to drop things wherever she felt like it sometimes. It had been a long day, both at work and at Gatsby's, and she needed a nice, soothing shower right now. She undressed, leaving a trail of clothes in the hall behind her before stepping into the bathroom and closing the door.

Outside, the driver's side back door of Barbara's Oldsmobile slowly opened, and George raised his head out for a look around. It confirmed what he had seen through the windows, that there were no other houses close enough for anyone to see him, and he was far enough off the road that there was little chance of a passing motorist spotting him as he made his way to the front door.

He tried the knob, and it was locked. No matter; even people who were careful about their front doors weren't always so conscientious when it came to the back ones. Sure enough, when he crept to the rear of the house, found a door and tried it, it opened easily.

As George stepped into the dark kitchen and carefully closed the door behind him, he heard a shower going. That pleased him; it would make things easier, just as it had with the young girl back at the apartment. He had caught her completely by surprise, and she had seemed more confused than scared just before he—

## NIGHTMARE

The sound of the shower suddenly stopped. George stopped too halfway across the kitchen, then went to a drawer and slowly opened it, inspecting its contents in the dim light from the living room. Nothing useful in here, so he went to the next one, and found what he needed. He withdrew the large butcher knife and held it close by his side. Now she'd be toweling herself off, or maybe she'd turn on a hair dryer, and either way she'd be distracted when he came for her.

He had just entered the hallway when a phone rang in the living room. It almost startled him, and as he saw the bathroom door start to open, he retreated into the kitchen. The woman walked down the hall, wrapped in a towel, right past him and into the living room, where she picked up the receiver.

George contemplated waiting, for if he struck while she was speaking to someone, that someone might hear something over the line, some tiny little audible clue that could come back to bite him later.

"Hello?" she said into receiver. A brief pause, then "Hello, Steve?" Another pause. "Steve, if that's you, I can't hear you."

George smiled. This was going to be easy after all. The woman looked at the receiver, then crouched down to hang it up. When she stood up, he was already upon her.

George brought up the butcher knife and sliced her throat open with one quick, decisive move. She let out a shocked gasp as he stepped away and watched her stagger across the room, clutching at the wound as it spewed blood down onto her clothes and out onto the floor in front of her. George could *hear* the blood as it splattered on the carpet, the sound mixing with her strangled gasps before she took another halting step and collapsed to the floor.

## MICHAEL GINGOLD

The visions came again, vivid but so quick that they did not interrupt him finishing the job. Rather, they almost seemed to guide him. As he went to the woman and turned her over onto her back, he saw a second of his mother *or maybe not* mounting his father and straddled the woman. Another flash of his father being slapped, and he plunged the knife into the woman's body. More blood spurted forth as he stabbed her *she slapped him* and stabbed her *she slapped him* and stabbed her, until the visions went away, quelled for now.

He looked down at her, her savaged throat still oozing red, the knife buried almost to the hilt in her abdomen. His head cleared, and he felt gratified that the urges were gone now. All that was left was the cleanup. And he had the time and means for this one, unlike the scene back at the apartment.

Putting his hands under her shoulders and lifting, George dragged the woman's body from the living room and down the hallway, over her abandoned clothes, leaving streaks of gore in her wake. He pulled her into the bathroom and dropped her into the tub. She could finish bleeding out there.

Removing the knife from her body was more difficult than he expected, but with a good yank, it came free, trailing a new stream of blood. He took it to the kitchen and ran it and his hands under hot water in the sink, using a good amount of dish detergent. There was no way he could sufficiently take care of the mess in the living room and hallway, but no body and the murder weapon lying spotless in the drawer would make an investigation a lot more difficult.

# THE THIRD DAY

**JACKSON HAD NOT**, in fact, found out about Tatum's disappearance until this morning. Not that that helped matters much. No word had come down to Dr. Williamson from anyone who had seen Tatum or knew where he was, and now Jackson was sitting in his office, one of his goddamn ever-present malodorous cigars in his mouth, looking through Tatum's file. It was a meaningless action; there was nothing in those pages that was going to help them find their errant patient. Jackson was just doing it to draw out the moment, which frustrated Dr. Williamson all the more. He just wanted to get the inevitable confrontation over with.

Finally, Jackson spoke. "The halfway house doesn't know where he is, the outpatient desk hasn't seen him . . . " He looked up, flipping the cigar in his mouth so it was pointed like a weapon at Dr. Williamson. "And you're his doctor and you don't know where the fuck he is, huh? That makes it kind of unanimous, doesn't it? Hmmmm?"

He closed the file, tossing it onto the desk. "No one, in fact, knows where he is?"

The questions were all rhetorical, and all Dr. Williamson could say was, "Look, for what it's worth, I'm sorry."

## MICHAEL GINGOLD

"Sorry?!" Jackson got to his feet, snatching the cigar from his mouth. "You lose a dangerously psychotic patient from a secret experimental drug program, and all you can say is 'Sorry'?!"

Now he looked like he wanted to stab Dr. Williamson with the cigar. "Did you check his job?"

Dr. Williamson couldn't help but hang his head. "Yeah. He left there two weeks ago."

"And nobody there thought to inform you of this? Nobody thought to inform anyone? Is there anyone involved in this case who knows their ass from their fucking elbow?"

"You know, I think we're making altogether too big a thing out of this." He was careful not to say "you're." "As far as I'm concerned, the man is simply not dangerous."

A withering pause before Jackson said, "You're a bigger schmuck than I thought you were. You do recall this is a guy who cut off another man's dick, right?"

"That was before the program. Tatum has made significant progress since then. You know that, you added all the information yourself to his report just the other day."

"He was controlled, Paul, not cured. I'd expect you to know the difference. Now he's out there God knows where, and even if he just so happens to have any of his meds, and if he just so happens to actually decide to take them, he's going to run out of them before long. And they're not the kind of drugs you can just pick up at a fucking Walgreens!"

Dr. Williamson was getting angry himself now. He didn't like being berated, especially when he was just as concerned about this case as Jackson was. He just wasn't prone to taking his frustrations out on other people. But he did have one retort he could throw back at Jackson.

## NIGHTMARE

"Look, I said from the beginning that we should have him housed somewhere more secure. And when Triumph Security offered to install that new system in the place we did have him, it was you who turned them down."

"It was an unproven system. I didn't trust those electronic locks any further than I could throw 'em."

"They've had them at The Haven since around the same time, and Leo Bain swears by them."

"Leo Bain should be locked up with his patients. And don't change the subject, Paul. You need to do something about this cockup, and I mean yesterday."

"What about you?"

"What about me? I've got the higher-ups to deal with on this. You're just lucky it's me instead of Cooper down here."

He took a puff on his cigar and blew the smoke at Dr. Williamson, who waved it away and sat down on the couch opposite his desk.

"I want him back," Jackson said, in a tone promising grave consequences if that didn't happen. "And if you value your job, you will get him back in this hospital before things get out of hand. Now, am I making myself perfectly clear to you? Do you get it?"

He knew he had to say something in reply, and all he came up with was, "Yes. I get it."

"Good." Jackson turned away from him, looking out the window, and made a grunt of disgust. "Get off your ass and find him."

\*\*\*

*The woman's severed head opened its eyes, staring dead at him, and it almost seemed like her head wasn't disembodied but just protruding from the bloody mattress, and that the rest of her was about to tear through it and—*

## MICHAEL GINGOLD

George awoke, but not screaming. That was some small relief, at least. As he lay in the bed, he briefly wondered, could it be that he was somehow getting used to the nightmares, like people with chronic pain who eventually learned to manage it and live their lives?

But as he lay there, practically naked in only his underwear, which only made him feel more vulnerable, he knew that wasn't the case. He had a sense of being paralyzed, held in place by the lingering chill left over from the dream. It was a sense he recalled from childhood, when he would have the occasional, very different kind of nightmare, and when he awoke, he was still so frightened that he couldn't move, lest he encounter whatever it was that had lurked in his dreamscape, and had somehow traveled with his consciousness into the dark of his bedroom, waiting to strike if he drew attention to himself.

But this room wasn't dark; it was morning, light streaming in through the window across the room. He hadn't bothered to draw the blinds, and he realized now that that had been a mistake . . .

Good. He was starting to think rationally now again. *Where am I?* he thought, then answered himself, *You're in a motel somewhere near Myrtle Beach. You found a place that was still open at that hour of the night, and were lucky enough that it was one where the desk clerk was happy to take cash, didn't ask you to sign in, didn't even ask for your name. Ordinarily, no one in their right mind would stay in a place like this—*

*But you're not in your right mind, are you?* another part of his brain taunted, and he pushed that thought away. Yes, he was, actually. He had taken very good care of the woman's body last night. Once the last

## NIGHTMARE

of her blood had flowed down the bathtub drain, he had carefully and thoroughly wrapped her body up in the shower curtain, and sealed the whole thing with duct tape he had found in a closet. Even if someone was standing right by the car outside, where the corpse lay in the trunk, they wouldn't be able to smell it. Hell, someone could be standing out there right now, and . . .

That thought made him first turn to face the window, then get up—which he was relieved to find he actually could—and approach it, trying to calm his breath, which was coming in ragged gasps. Outside, there was nobody standing around the parking lot, which was good. Nobody regarding the car suspiciously, and nobody to see him standing at the window in his Fruit of the Looms.

He closed the blinds and went over to what passed for a bathroom: a toilet behind a wall but without a door, a shower stall maybe big enough for a young child, and a sink/countertop with a mirror mounted over it. At least there were a couple of cheap drinking cups here, and he switched on the sickly green fluorescent light above the mirror, pulled the plastic wrapping off one cup and filled it from the tap, then picked up his pill bottle from the counter.

The bottle was a little less than half full, and he thought he was going to have to start conserving. But could he? Even one at a time, they'd be gone before long. He decided not to think about that just now, took two of the pills, and chased them with some water. His breathing slowed, and he felt he was getting himself under control, and he looked up into the mirror—

Where a young boy gazed back at him, his face streaked and clothes soaked in red. Stifling a cry, George looked back down at the sink, then up into the glass again. There the boy was again, staring back at

## MICHAEL GINGOLD

George, big splotches of blood on the wall behind him too, and George suddenly recognized the boy as himself.

And as the initial shock passed, George realized that the splattered, dripping crimson wasn't on the wall behind his younger self, but in front of him, on a mirror that the boy was looking into. George wasn't just seeing himself in the reflection, he was there in that other room; he *was* the boy, witnessing the aftermath of—

And then the vision was gone, and it was his own self back in the reflection, bathed in sweat.

His heart racing, George glanced quickly at the covered window, then pulled down his briefs and stepped into the tiny shower.

\*\*\*

Susan hung up her bedside phone with a sense of relief. Work had called to say that they were having problems with the power, and she didn't need to come in today. The kids had literally just gone out the door when the phone rang, and if the call had come just a minute or two later, she would have followed them and gotten all the way to the store before she found out the news. But this morning, timing had been on her side.

In fact, fate in general seemed to be smiling on her. The kids had been their usual unruly selves, but they had been squabbling with each other and hadn't directed any of their attitude at her. C.J. had even apologized right away after knocking a box of cereal all over the floor. She was still hoping that Bob could have that talk with C.J. that he had mentioned yesterday, but right now, she just wanted Bob for herself. That passionate afternoon on his boat had extended into the evening, and she was thrilled that it appeared an encore was possible today.

# NIGHTMARE

At times, she envied the life that being a freelance photographer allowed him; no workplace to show up to every day, a different experience with every job. Of course, there could be the uncertainty of where the next assignment was coming from, but he and his skills with the camera were admired and appreciated by so many people in the area that he always stayed busy. And yet not so busy that he couldn't make frequent time for her, and for the kids. A few months back, he had taken them all to SeaWorld, which had been a wonderful trip; Tammy and Kim still asked when they could go back and see Cindy and Sandy, the performing dolphins, again.

And yet, there was something of a rogue in him. When he had talked about being a pirate yesterday, she thought that in a sense, he wasn't kidding. There was a side of him that she could see setting sail on his boat and heading off to circle the globe. And there was a side of her that wanted to go with him, to take to the open ocean with just him, and leave the kids behind . . .

She pushed that fantasy aside, and fell back onto her bed. She half-considered just getting under the covers and dozing for a while, but there were better things to do with the time she now had. She picked up the phone and punched in a number.

Bob answered on the second ring. "Y-y-y-yello?"

"Hi, babe," she said. "Guess who doesn't have to go into work today?"

"Really? Well, that's great news. How do you plan on spending your day off?"

"Oh, I don't know. Do a bit of shopping, maybe go see a movie. Unless you can think of something better."

"I know I can." She could almost hear him smile over the phone. "So the kids are off to school?"

"Yes, yes. The kids have gone. No screaming kids all day."

"Good. Come on down, the boat is open and waiting for you."

"Is it now? Does it miss me?"

"I think it does. It was saying so just a few minutes ago."

"Well, I wouldn't want to disappoint it."

"Last night was very special for it. And it hopes it was special for you too."

"Of course last night was special."

"Then we'll see you soon?"

"Absolutely," she said, and blew a kiss into the phone. "Bye."

She hung up, and smiled at the ceiling. Then looked at the clock, and sat up. No sense lying around here when she could be lying around on Bob's boat, and she was already ready to go. She was in her car and on her way to the marina within minutes.

It was only when she pulled into the parking lot that she realized she had forgotten to leave the key under the front doormat for when the kids got home. No matter, she'd deal with that later. She wasn't going to think about that right now.

\*\*\*

"This is WWLA, Daytona Beach, with relaxing music from Love 95," the DJ intoned, and George smiled. He was relaxed, perhaps more so than he'd been in a long time. He'd left the motel at daybreak, and the woman behind the counter had barely looked up at him when he came in to check out. Clearly she'd been up all night, and was just waiting out the remaining time before her replacement came in and she could get some sleep. George thought he could be standing there with his clothes covered in blood, and she wouldn't notice.

Instead, those clothes were wrapped up securely in a garbage bag, stashed in the trunk with the

# NIGHTMARE

woman's body. After he'd thrown them in there, he'd taken the Oldsmobile and somehow found his way back to the dirt road, and his abandoned car, where he recovered the suitcase he'd left in there for so many months. The clothes inside now smelled a little moldy, of course, but it was nothing a good washing couldn't fix. The motel, no surprise, hadn't had the facilities for that, but he'd see to it—though not right away. He had other business to attend to.

As he pulled off Route 95 and onto 528, the sights were reassuringly familiar. He hadn't been down this road in so many years, but now it seemed like no time had passed. There was no need for a map; he knew exactly where he was going.

\*\*\*

The school bus doors hissed open, and C.J., Tammy, and Kim leaped from the exit and bolted to and up the driveway, books and folders under their arms. C.J. liked to make it a race, and acted as if he would always win because he was a boy. So sometimes, Tammy would put on a little extra speed and easily beat him to the front door.

Today, though, she couldn't be bothered with that, but she did run fast enough to be right behind him as he pulled open the screen door. Kim quickly joined them—and they quickly became jammed up when C.J. tried the front doorknob and found it wasn't open.

"It's locked," C.J. said, and duh, that was obvious, Tammy thought. They all called out "Mom!" and when they got no answer, they tried to peer in through the window on the door. But from what they could see, there was no one inside.

"Where is she?" C.J. asked. "I dunno," Tammy replied, and pushed him backward.

"What are you doing?"

"She must have left the key," Tammy said, and with herself and C.J. free of the mat, she picked it up, only to find nothing underneath.

"Well, where is it?" C.J. said, and Tammy sighed. "Obviously not there. She must have gone out and forgot."

"Then how do we get in?" Kim said, and Tammy pointed toward the side of the house. "Go check the other door."

Within seconds, Kim was back. "Nope."

"Wait," C.J. said, "I can get up this way."

He ran over to a drainpipe, dropping his books to one side. "Tammy, help me up here." He took hold of the pipe, and Tammy laced her fingers together, leaning down. He stepped into her hands, she gave him a boost and he began to climb. Then she thought of something and opened her hands, dropping C.J. awkwardly to the ground.

"What did you do that for?"

"You don't need my help. You can get up there just fine."

"What do you mean?"

"The other night. That was you on the roof, wasn't it?"

"No it wasn't!"

"Yes it was. You had a mask or something and you were looking at us."

"I wasn't looking at you. I was in bed the whole time!"

"You're such a liar. Well, you're not gonna scare me again because I'll know it's you!"

"It's not gonna be me because I didn't do it!"

"Never mind. Just get up there and let us in."

"Then give me a boost."

She didn't want to, because she wanted him to

# NIGHTMARE

admit it had been him who scared her and Kim, but she wanted more to just get inside. She joined her hands again, and he stepped into them and easily pulled himself up the pipe and onto the roof. He went to one of the second-floor windows and disappeared inside.

Tammy and Kim waited a few moments while nothing happened, and Tammy became annoyed again. She'd bet he was just going to stay in there and not let them in, to get back at her for figuring out his stupid prank. Well, if he did, she'd show him. With Kim's help, she could just as easily get up that drainpipe and—

The front door opened, C.J. standing innocently inside. "Come on," he beckoned, and the girls ran in past him. Just as she was about to head upstairs, Tammy turned and gave him a big smile. "Don't forget, C.J., Mom said you gotta take out the garbage!"

"No way!" C.J. retorted.

"Uh-huh! She said it, don't you remember, Kim?"

"Yep!" Kim called down from the top of the stairs.

"I'm not gonna do it just 'cause you say so."

"Okay, fine," Tammy said. "When she gets home, and she sees the garbage isn't out, you'll be in trouble 'cause she said you had to do it." Satisfied that she'd gotten him with her irrefutable logic, she headed up to her room.

C.J. stood in the living room, frowning. Of course, Mom had told him it was his turn to take out the garbage, but he didn't think Tammy had heard that. And his sister was right, of course—when Mom got back, which could be any minute now, she'd get mad if she saw it hadn't been done.

A couple of minutes later, C.J. came out the side door, the bag of trash about half his size slung over his shoulder. There was something sharp inside it pressing against his back, so he flipped it over and continued, but that didn't feel much better.

As he made his way to the curb, he got a strange feeling, like he wasn't alone even though there was nobody else out there. He stopped and looked back at the house, expecting to see Tammy watching from the door or a window, gloating. But there was no one.

Picking up speed, he reached the curb and was about to drop the bag. And that's when the man stepped out from behind a tree just down and across the main road, no more than 20 feet away.

C.J. stopped suddenly, taken by surprise even though he'd had a feeling someone was there. The man was dressed in a trenchcoat, and regarded him curiously, making C.J. think maybe he was a detective checking him out. Could it be because of Kathy calling the police the other night? Did they know it was him on the roof, and they were watching him now?

But no. There was something strange about this man. Something in the way he was looking at C.J. He wasn't regarding him with suspicion, it was more like... well, C.J. couldn't tell exactly what it was. It was almost like the man was studying him, trying to memorize him.

C.J. dropped the bag to the curb, but kept a hand on it. It wasn't like the bag or the trash inside would protect him much if the man turned out to be dangerous, but it made him feel just a little bit safer to be holding onto *something*. Part of him wanted to just turn and run, but what if the man followed? It was just him and his sisters; if the man tried to get in the house and go after them, who would protect them?

And so C.J. stood there, staring back at the man, trying to be brave. The man wasn't moving, but maybe if C.J. stared at him long enough, he'd go away . . .

# NIGHTMARE

\*\*\*

Susan lay on the bunk below decks in Bob's boat, trying to enjoy the afterglow, even though the kids were still on her mind. The sex had been great, and now Bob was caressing her back the way she liked. She thought she could just lie like this for a few hours, but the time to get home was fast approaching.

And also, Bob might want to go for another round, like he often did. Sure enough, he gently lifted her head and started kissing her, passionately enough that she knew he was going for take two.

"You're waking me up," he murmured, which seemed like an odd thing to say. She rested her head back on the pillow, and he went back to running his hands over her, while kissing her neck.

It felt nice, very nice, but she looked up at her watch lying beside the bunk and knew she couldn't get back into it. Not now.

"Susan, let's go again," he whispered in her ear, as if his intentions weren't already obvious.

"No time," she said, and checked the watch. By now, the bus would be just about to drop the kids off, if it hadn't already. "I've got to go."

"So soon?"

"Yeah, the kids will be back home any minute, and I forgot to leave them the key."

She started to get up, and he kissed her again. "They can fend for themselves. They can wait at the neighbors'."

Both of those were true, and they probably would be fine if she was a little late . . . but no. Right now, she felt she needed to be there for them.

"I'm sorry, I have to get home, I really do. Where's my sweater?"

She found it on the floor, half under the bunk, and

quickly put it on. Her pants were all the way underneath, and she retrieved them as Bob just laid there, putting on an aggrieved face.

"Come on," he said as she finished dressing. And as she headed for the stairs: "Woman, you are torturing me! I have needs!"

She knew he was joking, or at least half-joking. He would sometimes playfully cajole her where sex was concerned, but never pressure her. And on many occasions, she would give in after a bit of teasing, but this situation was different.

She found the phone on the upper deck, and as Bob called out, "I'm a human being! I've got feelings!" she punched in her number. Just in case they had found their way inside. She wouldn't put it past C.J. to know how to get in in the absence of a key.

It rang several times, and Susan was about to hang up when there was a soft click, followed by "Hello?" It was Kim, and she sounded anxious and upset.

"Kim?" Susan said, immediately concerned.

"Mom, is this you?" The pitch of the girl's voice raised several levels. "Mom, please, hurry home! Hurry home!"

"Kim, please, stop screaming. I know I'm not home. I'll be there in five minutes."

"Mom! Mom!" Susan could hear Tammy screaming in the background too, and she could feel her heart starting to race. "What's going on there?"

Kim said nothing, and for an awful moment Susan thought the call was about to get cut off. Then Tammy, in the background but as clear is if she was standing right beside her: "Mom, it's C.J.! He's on the floor covered in blood!"

"He's what?" But Susan had heard exactly what she said, and a wave of panic struck her. "Don't touch him, okay? Neither of you! I'll be right there!"

# NIGHTMARE

"Please, he's got blood all over him! I don't know what happened!"

"You just stay there! I'm coming right now!"

She hung up, and Bob emerged from below decks, fully clothed, any amorous thoughts long gone. "What's wrong, what's going on?"

"It's C.J.! It's C.J.!" Sobbing now, she pushed past him, grabbed her purse and made for the dock.

"Well, give me the keys, I'll drive you over."

"No, I just have to go!"

"Honey," he said, catching up to her. "You're in no state to drive. Let me take you, come on."

She stopped for a moment, relenting. Digging into the purse, she came up with the keys and thrust them into his hand. Then she jumped onto the dock and ran for the parking lot.

Bob caught up to her just as she reached the car. He let her in the passenger side, then jumped into the driver's seat. Backing out into the road with barely a notice of whether anyone was coming, he sped toward the house.

Susan was crying uncontrollably now, and Bob searched for the words to try to calm her.

"Now tell me, what exactly did C.J. say?"

"He didn't say anything! It was Kim, and Tammy. They said he was lying on the floor, and he had blood all over him!"

He suddenly knew there was one good explanation, one that would console her right away. But he didn't want to say it just now, in case it turned out he was wrong.

"Did they say if he was conscious?"

"No, I just told you, all they said was he was covered in blood!"

She was getting hysterical now. "Okay, just calm

down. You're not going to be any help to C.J. if you're a nervous wreck. We'll be there any minute."

"That might not matter! He could already . . . be . . ."

"He isn't, okay? Listen, you don't know what's wrong with him, and there's no sense in getting all upset till we get there."

And as they turned onto Indian River Drive, only minutes from the house, he just hoped he was right.

\*\*\*

C.J. lay on the floor, groaning, as Tammy tried to look under his red-soaked shirt to see how badly he was hurt.

"Leave me alone!" he screamed, his breathing hoarse and heavy.

"Tell me what happened!" Tammy pleaded.

"It hurts! Let me be!"

"Let me see!" She reached for his shirt again, and he slapped her hand away.

"Leave me alone, I said!"

"Tell me what happened!" she repeated. "Did somebody do this to you?"

"Just don't touch me!"

Tammy looked around with frightened eyes, hoping Kim was still there. It would make her feel a little better if she was. But Kim was gone. Tammy hadn't heard or seen her go upstairs; maybe she went outside to wait for Mom. She turned back to C.J., who was quietly whimpering now.

"C.J., if you'll just let me see . . ."

"I told you, leave me alone!"

Kim was, in fact, sitting out by the driveway, looking anxiously down the road. After what seemed like forever, she saw their car approaching, and stood up. The passenger door flew open, and Kim ran to Susan as she jumped out.

# NIGHTMARE

"Mom, Mom! He's dying, he's dying!"

Susan embraced her as Bob flew out of the driver's side and ran for the house. He burst through the door, Susan and Kim right behind him—and stopped short as he took in the scene at the foot of the stairs.

Susan hadn't been exaggerating; the bottom half of C.J.'s untucked white shirt was soaked in blood, which streaked his pants as well. Tammy sat beside him, and when she turned, Bob saw a tear slide down from one eye.

"Oh, shit," he said, as C.J. groaned. "Oooohhhhhh, it hurts . . ."

"Out of the way, quick!" Bob gently pushed past Tammy and leaned down over C.J. The boy was clutching his stomach with hands as coated in blood as his clothes.

"Just relax, C.J., we're here now," Bob said as Susan crouched down beside him. "Everything's going to be all right. Just lift your head up, just a little bit, okay?"

He brushed C.J.'s hair aside to get a better look at his face. The poor kid seemed on the verge of passing out.

"Now just tell me what happened. Tell us what happened, C.J. How did you get like this?"

C.J.'s breathing slowed just a bit, and looked up at Bob weakly and said, "A man . . ."

"A man? What man?"

"Out by . . . the street. He tried to kill me with a knife."

"Oh my God," Susan stammered. *How could this happen?* her mind screamed. *How could someone just attack my child, almost kill him, in broad daylight? In front of his own house??*

"It hurts. Oh, Mommy, it hurts!"

"It's okay, buddy," Bob said. "You're gonna be okay. I'm here, your mommy's here, we're all here now. We're gonna take care of you, it's gonna be all right. Just let me see . . ."

He started to gently pull C.J.'s hands from his stomach, but the boy resisted. Now that doubt was starting to creep into Bob's mind again, and he thought he caught the trace of a familiar smell . . .

"It hurts!" C.J. groaned, and Bob took the boy's hands in his a little tighter.

"I'm not gonna hurt you. It's gonna be all right, I just need to lift up your shirt. Like I said, I'm not gonna hurt you."

There was a little more resistance, but then C.J. let Bob move his hands away and lift his shirt.

Bob saw that while the garment was steeped in red, there wasn't nearly as much on C.J. himself. His body only bore traces of it, with no visible wound. And when Bob got some of the "blood" on his hands, the consistency confirmed what he had suspected all along.

He rubbed it between his fingers, then tasted it. Susan looked confused, and a little disgusted, by that, but what it brought to Bob was relief, touched by a bit of anger.

And as an uncontrollable smile spread across C.J.'s face, Bob turned to Susan and said, "It's ketchup."

C.J. started laughing, and it was a laugh that turned Susan's panic into fury. It wasn't just that he thought his prank was funny; Susan could tell that C.J. thought her fear, her *concern* for him, for God's sake, was funny.

Bob put an arm around her shoulders, but she shook it off.

## NIGHTMARE

"I knew it. I knew it!"

"No you didn't," C.J. said softly, with a giggle.

"Yes I did. I could see it in your eyes!" She was on her feet now, pointing accusingly at her son. "I've had it! I've had it with these tricks! You just love to scare all of us, don't you? We could have had an accident out there driving so fast, but you don't care about that, do you? You don't care about your own mother, or anyone but yourself! Get upstairs to bed!"

"But it's not even 4 . . ."

"I don't care! Get upstairs, I mean it! I don't want to even see you for the rest of the night! Don't come down till tomorrow morning, either!"

C.J. got to his feet and hurried up the stairs. Susan pushed past Bob into the kitchen, where she dropped roughly into one of the chairs. A couple of half-eaten sandwiches sat on plates on the table, along with the peanut butter and jelly jars, still open, not put away.

Bob approached her from behind, Tammy and Kim standing a few feet back, watching nervously.

"Hey, that's your boy," Bob said. "He's a little too bright and a little too imaginative . . ."

"Imaginative? Is that what you call what just happened?"

Bob had no answer, so Susan continued.

"Trying to make us think he'd been stabbed, he was dying? Saying some . . . man outside attacked him? That's not 'imaginative,' Bob. That's something else. No normal boy is that obsessed with blood, and scaring people."

"He's not some kind of gangster. He just . . . has an unconventional way of expressing himself."

"Listen to you. You sound like one of those people who go on TV after somebody kills someone, and says, 'I can't understand, he seemed perfectly normal'!"

"Susan, has C.J. ever actually hurt anyone?"

That stopped her for a moment. She had to admit, he was right about that. Nothing C.J. had done had ever caused harm to anybody. But still, that didn't excuse what had just happened.

"No, he hasn't. But that's not the point." She turned to look at the girls, who were hovering behind Bob in the hallway. "And as for you two . . . Tammy, you're the oldest, now you should know better."

"How was I supposed to know he was faking?" She sounded on the verge of bursting into tears herself.

"Don't be so hard on them, they . . . " Bob said, and Susan fixed him with a glare that told him not to continue.

Then, to the girls, she snapped, "Just get in the television room, I don't even want to see you right now. Just go in there and watch something."

Tammy and Kim retreated without another word. Susan abruptly stood up and grabbed one of the plates, using a knife to scrape one partial sandwich onto the other.

"Look at this mess." She called out after the departed girls. "How many times do I have to tell you to clean up after yourselves, huh?"

She picked up the other plate, went to the kitchen trash can and scraped the remains of the sandwiches into it. One came apart, the peanut butter keeping it stuck to the plate, and with a grunt of anger she dumped the whole thing into the can, followed by the knife.

"Hey, relax." Bob stepped up behind her. "Just mellow out."

She whirled on him. "What do you know? You don't have to face this every day!"

Susan stalked into the little sitting room off the

kitchen, and sat down on the couch. Bob was about to say that he wouldn't mind facing it every day, and being even more a part of the kids' lives—but that would spark a whole other argument, because there was only a part of him that wanted that and he knew it, and she knew it too.

"I hate this fucking house," she said, quieter now but still seething. "Do you know, I've hated this house since the day he left?"

"Then leave." He'd suggested that before, but for whatever reason the answer was always—

"It's not that easy," she said. "You know that."

"Not really." He looked around. "It's paid for. You could sell it."

"And go where? The state this house is in, where would I find another one with room for the four of us?"

"I don't know. But when was the last time you looked? Four years ago, five?"

She said nothing, because he was right.

"And it's in fine shape. I can help straighten up for someone to come look at it. Why don't you call Compass Points and go down there?"

"Maybe." She looked away, and he tried another tactic. "You want a drink?"

Silence for a moment, then: "Scotch is in the bar."

As soon as she said it, he was already headed for the bar in the living room. He poured a Scotch for Susan and one for himself, and brought them into the sitting room. Taking a seat beside her, he handed her one glass, and she knocked back half of it as he took a sip.

"We've got to do something about him," she said.

"What did you have in mind?"

"Some kind of therapy, maybe. I know you're right, little boys like to play pranks, but the things he's been doing . . . There's something wrong with him, Bob."

"Does his school have some kind of counselor he can talk to?"

"I don't know. I'll have to ask them."

"Or maybe they can recommend someone."

"I hope so. He won't talk to me about it. Every time I bring it up, he just shuts down."

"Look, I'm not trying to criticize, but if you're upset when you talk to him . . . "

"I'm not always upset!" She realized immediately how that sounded, and said more quietly, "I do try to talk to him normally, to reason with him, but nothing works."

"Well, like I said, I can try talking to him. I'm not a professional, but I was a little boy once."

"Thank you." She finished her drink, and abruptly changed the subject. "I just can't believe it. The day after C.J. was born. Who abandons their family the day after the birth of their child?"

"Honey, you're never going to know that. It's nine years, you have to let that go."

"I know I do. But this would be so much easier if he was here."

"Hey." She looked up at him. "I'm here. And I'll do everything I can to help you through this."

"Thank you." They kissed quickly, and he smiled. The storm had passed.

"Tell you what. You know what'll make everything better? Going out to McDuff's and getting some fish."

She couldn't help but laugh. "That'll make everything better?"

"I promise." He stood, stepped into the kitchen and called down the hall, toward the sounds of a cartoon on the TV. "Hey girls! Feel like going out to McDuff's to get some fish?"

# NIGHTMARE

An enthusiastic "Yes!" and "Yay!" came back. "Okay, turn off the tube and get ready!"

He walked back in to Susan. "Want me to go and get C.J.?"

"No. He can stay here. I told him he's grounded, and he's grounded."

"Okay. Does that mean we're not taking him to the launch?"

"Oh, shit. I forgot that was tonight." She had promised the kids they could go down to the beach later on and watch the satellite launch. C.J. had been anxiously awaiting it for weeks, and though she felt like missing it would be a punishment that would stick with him, she now thought that all it would do was foster even more resentment, and just make the problem worse. Making him stay home while the rest of them went out to dinner would be enough for now, she decided.

"I guess we can still take him to that. But he stays here for now."

A few minutes later, C.J. watched from his bedroom window as Tammy and Kim ran toward the car, ahead of his mother and Bob. They got in, Bob driving again, and the car backed down the driveway and disappeared down the road.

C.J. closed the curtain and flopped back onto his bed. They were going without him. It wasn't surprising; when he heard Bob yell to Tammy and Kim that they were going out, he knew better than to go downstairs to try to join them. It would just make Mom madder, and as mad as he was at her, he hoped that she'd be in a better mood when they got home, and he could go with them to see the rocket launch that night.

So now it was just him, left to eat whatever he

## MICHAEL GINGOLD

could find in the fridge while the rest of them stuffed themselves with School o' Fish Platters at McDuff's. This was happening so often now, ever since Mom started seeing Bob. Sure, Tammy and Kim were usually at home with him, along with Kathy, doing her best to keep him and his sisters out of trouble. But he didn't want Kathy there so much. He wanted his mom, for her to spend more nights with them instead of being out with Bob all the time.

It wasn't like that with Mom's other boyfriends. Pete, the one before Bob, had also taken her for regular evenings out to dinner or whatever, but she was usually back in time to put him and his sisters to bed. He had heard Mom on the phone sometimes with her friends, wondering why Pete never wanted to have her spend much time at his place. And then, all of a sudden, Mom stopped seeing Pete. He had asked her why once, but she just said that it didn't work out between them and that was that. And the few times after that he had come upon her talking on the phone with someone about Pete, she had quickly changed the subject when she saw he was there.

So now it was Bob, who obviously had no problem letting Mom spend a lot of time on his boat. He wasn't a bad guy, really, and had done some nice things for them all, like the trip to SeaWorld, and the time he had gotten them into part of the Kennedy Space Center after he'd taken some pictures there. But in the last few months, Mom had been spending more and more time with him, and it seemed like she was more interested in that than in being with him and his sisters.

And now today, she had gone off with him and left the house locked up so they couldn't get in. Then that strange man had shown up, looking at him, almost like he had been waiting for C.J. He had just walked away

## NIGHTMARE

after a few minutes, but what if he *had* attacked C.J. with a knife? What if he really had been badly hurt, covered with blood, and Mom wasn't there to take care of him? Well, maybe today she'd learned her lesson. Maybe after this, she'd try to be home more often and not off with Bob all the time.

He reached under the mattress and pulled out one of his monster magazines, the ones Mom didn't want him to have. She also didn't want him watching scary movies on TV, so the magazines were the next best thing. Fortunately the guy at the pharmacy just a 10-minute walk away didn't mind selling him the magazines at all. *He* didn't mind C.J. looking at scary stuff.

As he pored through the pages, taking in the images of Frankenstein's Monster, The Mummy and their kin, giggling every so often at the silly puns in the photo captions, his stomach started to rumble. Time to get something to eat. He stashed the magazine back in its hiding place, and was halfway down the stairs when the phone rang.

He stopped for a moment, pondering whether to answer it. He had a feeling it was Mom calling to check on him, and he thought that maybe he wouldn't pick up, just so she'd really know how he felt about being left behind. But then he remembered the rocket launch again, and ran down to the phone and picked up.

"Hello?"

He could tell someone was at the other end; he could vaguely hear breathing on the otherwise silent line. For a second he thought it might be one of his friends, but then he thought it sounded older, heavier.

"Hello?" he repeated. At that, even the breathing stopped, and there was nothing but silence. A moment later, there was a *click* and the line went dead.

C.J. shrugged, put the phone back in its cradle and went into the kitchen.

\*\*\*

George sat on the floor of the hotel room, the phone on one of the beds beside him. She still wasn't home, it seemed. Or maybe she was, and just left the boy to answer. He thought he might go back over there, just to be sure, but then pushed that thought away. He had somewhere else he had to go tonight, another woman he had to attend to.

He looked to the window, where the closed Venetian blinds let in just a few thin shafts of magic-hour light. It would be dark soon, and then time to go out.

\*\*\*

Jackson walked into his office, absently pushing the door shut behind him. He heard metal softly touch metal, but it didn't fully close, which was fine because it was late enough that no one was likely to disturb him.

He picked his satchel up off his desk, rifled through it and came up with a folder. When he opened it, the first thing that greeted him was an 8x10 of Tatum. Yeah, like that was necessary. This guy was consuming his life right now, and he was looking forward to the time when he would never have to look at that face again.

Behind that was a schedule sheet from Tatum's job, with a handwritten list of notations:

1. Mon—2 On Time
2. Wed—4 Late—5 mins.
3. Fri—6 On Time

# NIGHTMARE

4. Mon-9 Late-8 mins.
5. Wed-11 On time
6. Fri-13 No Show
7. Mon-16 No Show
8. Wed-18 No Show
9. Fri-20

It ended there, but Jackson didn't need to see any more. Those three "No Shows" in a row, each circled in red, told him everything he needed to know. The idiots had had a record of Tatum skipping out on work, but for whatever reason, they had decided to keep it to themselves.

He could feel his anger rising, and tamped it down. That horse had left the barn, and there was nothing left for them but the repercussions, which Jackson was going to make damn sure were severe. He closed the file, put it on his desk, and walked over to the window.

Half the windows in the buildings before him were dark, and as he watched, a couple of others winked out. He looked down at the street, and the streetlights illuminating the pedestrians. *They're safe, at least*, he thought, and wherever Tatum was, if they were lucky, really lucky, he would be tracked down quickly and this whole mess could be buried and forgotten about.

That thought had barely entered his mind when he heard the door shut behind him. He looked up, but didn't turn, because what he saw in the glass stopped him.

Cooper had entered the room without him hearing and closed the door, and now his reflection was looking evenly at Jackson from the window. He was a tall African-American man, dressed impeccably, with a steely gaze that made Jackson reluctant to turn around.

He took the cigar from his mouth and said to the reflection, "Come on in. Make yourself comfortable."

"I'm not comfortable, Jackson. Are you?"

Knowing he had no choice, Jackson turned to face him. Now Cooper was wearing that condescending smile he had seen too many times before, the one that made him feel like a kid who'd been called on by the teacher and didn't know the answer. "Would it help if I told you we're doing our best to fix this?"

"It would if by 'we,' you mean my team. Because we're the ones devoting resources we shouldn't be to finding this man."

"Believe me, I'm as upset about this as you are. This whole situation has been one fuck-up after—"

"I doubt very much you can comprehend how upset about this I am. He was your patient, and never mind the tests and the sessions, and everything else. Your greatest responsibility was making sure he stayed put. I'm told you turned down an offer from Triumph Security to assure his residence was more restrictive."

At that moment, Jackson hated Dr. Williamson. For being right.

"We evaluated the offer, and didn't believe it was necessary."

"Do you believe it was now?"

Neither answer would placate Cooper, and Jackson was suddenly at a loss for what to say next—a feeling he always hated, but especially with this guy. Finally, he decided to take a big gulp of his pride.

"I appreciate everything your team is doing to help. And I promise I'm going to keep doing everything I can."

"I hope so. Because you do realize that if he does

# NIGHTMARE

something . . . conspicuous, and people start looking into his history, we have a vested interest in making sure that trail ends here."

"You think I don't know that? I told you when we started, Cooper, we would take full responsibility for the program's success or failure."

"This is more than a failure, Jackson. Or it threatens to be."

He took a couple of steps forward, and Jackson had to resist the urge to back up. "And you told me a lot of things. You told me that out of all the potential candidates, he was the most likely to respond to the program. The most likely to have his psychopathology cured."

"And I stand by that diagnosis. Even now."

"Hmm. You know, I didn't bring this up before, because it wasn't really germane. But when I looked over the other potential subjects—the ones you considered less curable, and thus one would assume a greater danger—they all had one thing in common. Do you recall what it was?"

"Tatum was determined to psychologically be the best candidate for the program, and for your purposes," Jackson said, as evenly and forcefully as he could.

"That's not what I asked." Cooper let the silence hang in the air for several seconds before continuing. "You can say it, Jackson. It's just one word. It starts with a 'b'—"

"Hey!" Jackson was legitimately angry now. "That had nothing to do with his selection. And I don't appreciate you painting me as some kind of bigot."

"There's only one kind, Jackson. When you get right down to it."

There was another uncomfortable silence, and

## MICHAEL GINGOLD

Cooper stepped right up to him. "But that's neither here nor there. Right now, what you need to be concerned with is that your dog slipped the leash. And it's not going to be long before he makes a mess."

Jackson looked him in the eye—which wouldn't be so awkward if Cooper wasn't a head taller than him. "I swear on my family, and my job, that we will get him back."

"Then take comfort in the fact that you'll still have at least one when this is all over."

Cooper let that statement hang in the air a bit before turning to go. He was reaching for the door when Jackson, who couldn't let this fun little get-together end on that note, asked him, "Is that all you came down here for? To tell me what I already know?"

Cooper looked back toward him. That damn smile again. "I wanted to impress it upon you personally. To make sure you fully understand the consequences. And it appears it worked."

Damn it, he had hoped it wouldn't show on his face. Very few people intimidated Jackson, but this man...

Cooper stepped out as quietly as he had come in, closing the door behind him just hard enough to put one last bit of punctuation on the meeting. Jackson replaced the cigar in his mouth and went back to the window. *Just 10 minutes,* he thought. *Just 10 minutes earlier and I would have been out of here before he showed up...*

The thought trailed off. He knew that Cooper had been watching and waiting for the moment when he could confront him alone. And Cooper was right.

He did understand the consequences, and understood them fully.

\*\*\*

## NIGHTMARE

C.J. lay on his bed, engrossed in his magazine again. He didn't know why his mom and his sisters were taking so long; it was long after dark now, and they would have to leave soon if they wanted to get a good spot to watch the launch. Maybe after McDuff's, they had gone over to Friendly's to get some ice cream. They just better not have decided to go straight to the beach without him, or he would be—

His thoughts were interrupted by a sharp *tap* at his window. He looked up curiously, then realized what it was. He went to the window and opened it, just in time to stop Tony Walker from throwing another pebble at the glass.

Tony stood among the trees and shrubbery at the side of the house, holding a small padded envelope, wearing that Superman shirt he seemed to have on every other day. He was C.J.'s best friend, the only person C.J. felt he could always rely on. And so he was here, just as he had promised that day at school.

"C.J.? I'm here!" C.J. could see that, but Tony was always saying things that were already obvious. It made C.J. laugh inside sometimes, but Tony was a good enough friend that he wouldn't laugh to his face about it.

"What's up, Tony?"

"What do you think? I got your stuff!"

"Why didn't you just ring the doorbell?"

"Isn't your mom home?"

"Naw, she went out with Bob and my sisters for dinner. They'll be back any time, though."

"Oh. Why didn't you go with them?"

"I'm being punished."

"Oh." He didn't bother asking why. "Well then, come down!"

"You better just throw it up. Like I said, they'll be here any minute."

## MICHAEL GINGOLD

Tony tossed the envelope up to him, and C.J. caught it easily.

"Thanks! See you tomorrow."

"I'll see ya, bye!" Tony said before running off. C.J. watched him go—and sure enough, just as Tony disappeared into the distance, he heard the sound of an engine, and headlights swung across the spot where Tony had been standing a minute ago.

C.J. retreated into his room, and opened the envelope. He smiled when he saw what was inside, then pulled open a drawer as he heard the front door open, and his mom and sisters' voices. As he stuffed the envelope deep inside, down under his shirts, he thought they all sounded happy, and hoped that meant his mom was in a good mood, and he'd be joining them later.

\*\*\*

The satellite launch had originally been announced for the previous week, but an issue with the Atlas-Centaur rocket that would be carrying it had postponed the liftoff. The extra anticipation resulting from the delay meant that a slightly larger than usual crowd of families and tourists were gathered on the beach to watch the satellite head for the heavens.

C.J. was happy to be among them. Mom had in fact been in a forgiving frame of mind when she got home, so he had been on his best behavior too, not telling her that there hadn't been much in the fridge for him to have dinner, even though he wanted to.

And now they were all standing on the sand amongst other onlookers, peering toward the lights of the Cape Canaveral Air Force Station, waiting for the show. If it was anything like the others, it would only last about five minutes or so, but it would still be pretty cool.

# NIGHTMARE

C.J. just wished Bob didn't have to come with them. Couldn't he have watched it from his boat or something? When they'd gone to see rockets take off before, it had just been him and Mom and his sisters, but now Bob was there too, and they were holding hands and smiling at each other, and didn't seem to be noticing him or Tammy or Kim much.

In fact, when a couple of tall people walked over and took places in front of them, making it hard to see the Station clearly, neither Mom nor Bob seemed to notice until Tammy tugged on Mom's sleeve.

"Mom," she said, and Susan looked down. "What's up, hon?"

Tammy motioned to the couple and said quietly, "I can't see. Can we move?"

Susan looked quickly at Bob and replied, "Why don't the three of you go a little further down? Just stay together, okay?"

"Okay," Tammy said brightly, and she and Kim started to make their way toward the front of the assembled group.

C.J. hesitated for a moment. Of course Mom wanted them to move further up; it was just so she and Bob could be alone together. He thought he'd just stay put, but then Mom turned to him. "Make sure you stay with your sisters. Don't run off."

Fine. So she expected him to go too, and he decided not to argue and followed Tammy and Kim as they weaved their way through the other people, finding a spot at the edge of the group, closer to the water. The girls sat down, but C.J. remained standing.

"I'm gonna go a little further," he said, and Tammy frowned.

"Mom said we were supposed to stay together."

"I'll come right back after it takes off. Promise."

"Don't go, C.J.," Kim chimed in. "You're gonna get us in trouble."

"You won't get in trouble. If I'm not back right away, just say I had to go to the bathroom in the bushes."

"Ew, C.J., that's gross."

"I'm not gonna go far. Promise," he said again, and took off before they could object any more. He just wanted to get away from them all, be by himself, and enjoy the launch without having to think about his family.

At first, he kept his promise and didn't stray too far away. When he stopped and looked back, he could still vaguely see the others in the moonlight, and hear the low murmur of their conversations, broken by an occasional loud laugh. He decided he could go a little bit further, until he was just far enough away that he couldn't see or hear them. Then once the glow of the rocket was disappearing into the night sky, he would hurry back, and hopefully catch up to the girls before Mom noticed he had gone.

He walked another few minutes, until the sound of the group slipped away, replaced by the soft roar of the water rushing up the sand, then receding. It was calming to C.J., and he felt he'd found just right place to stop, sit down, and watch the launch undisturbed.

Just as he was about to take his seat on the sand, he heard another sound, from further down the beach. One he hadn't expected, since he didn't think anyone else was down here.

It was the metallic *thunk* of a car trunk being slammed shut.

At least, that's what it sounded like to C.J., but as he peered down in that direction, he couldn't see any cars. Which made sense, because he knew there were

# NIGHTMARE

no parking lots at this end of the beach. It was just woods, which meant that someone would have had to drive off the road and—

That's when he saw the figure making its way out of the trees and down onto the sand. It was moving strangely, and with the distance and the dim light, C.J. could barely even tell if it was human.

He wished he had brought the binoculars, but they were back with Mom and Bob. So he ran toward the shape staggering across the beach, being careful not to make any sound or to slip on the unstable sand beneath his feet.

The figure stopped, so he stopped too. But now he was close enough to see that it was . . . not one person, but two. It was someone carrying another, and from the looks of it, the head and legs dangling limply, the person being carried was—

C.J. gasped as he realized what he was witnessing. The air around him suddenly became colder as he crouched down, unable to tear his eyes away from the sight, or to turn and run. As frightened as he was now, he was also fascinated, and as long as he wasn't seen . . .

The figure dropped to a kneeling position, letting the corpse fall out of its arms. A woman's corpse, as C.J. got a quick glimpse of its long hair before it hit the sand. Now the figure was hunched over, head down. C.J. couldn't tell for sure, but it looked like it was shaking a little. Was it crying? Shivering, maybe, from the nighttime cold? That didn't seem likely, because as C.J.'s eyes further adjusted to the darkness, he could see that it was wearing a trenchcoat, and—

Now he was shivering as the shock of realization hit him. It was the man from before, the one who had stared at him from across the street. C.J. couldn't see his face, but he knew it, knew it for sure. And now he had killed someone, and was going to throw the body into the ocean, or maybe bury it out here.

He knew he should jump up and flee, to bolt back to his Mom and everyone else and tell them what was happening, to get help before the man finished his task and disappeared. Yet he was frozen in place, unable to tear his eyes away from the scene in front of him, frightened by what he was seeing—while that small part of him was also completely engrossed by it, anxious to see what would happen next.

The man looked up, out toward the ocean. He moved as if he was about to pick up the body again and continue toward the water. And that's when the rumbling began.

Both the man and C.J. turned their eyes toward the Station, and the glow issuing from it as the rocket began to rise. The roar became louder as it ascended, trailing a streak of fire, and the ground under C.J.'s feet started to tremble. For a moment, C.J. was distracted from his fear by the spectacle. Even though he had seen them before, the sights and sounds of the launches were always powerful enough to—

And then he heard the scream. It wasn't a scream of terror or discovery; no one had joined C.J. and spotted the man and his victim, now lit up by the fireball rising toward the stars. It was a howl of pure madness, and it was coming from the man himself.

A fresh chill ran through C.J.'s body as the scream continued, as if the infernal light and booming noise had shocked the man into insanity. Or furthered whatever madness was already there. As C.J. watched, the man turned away from the rising craft, his scream slowly dying, and his face finally became visible in the glow.

It *was* him. As if there had been any doubt before,

## NIGHTMARE

and even though he was some distance away, C.J. recognized him clearly as the man who had confronted him. He had been creepy enough in daylight, but out here in the night, he was a hundred times worse.

Could the man see him? Would he recognize C.J. and come after him, knowing that his crime had been observed? C.J. wondered if he could even outrun the man, who was taller and no doubt so much faster, and make it back to safety.

For a few more unbearable seconds, the man seemed to be staring right at him. Then, as the rocket and its light began to disappear from view, the man turned back toward the corpse beside him.

In an instant, C.J. was on his feet, dashing madly back toward the crowd, the sand tricky beneath him. He hadn't gotten far before it tripped him up, and he slammed down onto his stomach, the wind knocked out of him. He lay there gasping, knowing he needed to get back up and keep running, but the empty hole where his lungs should be wouldn't let him.

Twisting his body, he looked back down the beach. From here, in this position, he couldn't see where the man had been, but the man himself also wasn't visible, and that was good. He wasn't coming after C.J.—at least for the moment.

Finally, he found the strength to stand, and keep running.

As he approached the place where the people had been gathered, he could see that most of them were gone or starting to leave. There were four standing together who were not moving, though, two big and two small, and even before he could recognize them, C.J. knew there was going to be trouble. He picked up his pace, trying to run even faster, as if getting to them a few seconds earlier would make any difference.

## MICHAEL GINGOLD

"Where have you been?" Susan snapped before he had even reached them. "I told you to stay with your sisters!"

"I had to go to the bathroom. Didn't Tammy tell you?"

"How far did you go? You've been gone for the last 20 minutes!"

How did she know that? It certainly hadn't been 20 minutes since the launch. Then C.J. saw the binoculars hanging from their strap around Tammy's neck, and he realized. Mom and Bob must have come down to the girls to give them the binoculars just after he had left.

He still thought he had a good excuse. "I had to go further down the beach. I didn't want anyone to see me!"

"You shouldn't have gone at all! You should have just held it in. Running off down there in the middle of the night, what if something happened and you got hurt? What if we couldn't find you?"

"But I didn't! I'm fine, nothing happened!" He considered telling them what he had seen, but with Mom already as mad as she was, he knew she wouldn't believe him. And even if she did, it would just prove her point—that going down the beach had been dangerous. It would help her win the argument, and C.J. didn't want that.

"It could have happened, C.J., that's the point. What am I going to do with you? I said you could come tonight and let you off being grounded, and this is how you thank me?"

"Mom, I'm okay! It's no big deal." And then, thankfully, Bob chimed in. "He's fine, Susan. Nothing happened. Let's not blow this out of proportion."

Susan gave him a look that suggested blowing it

# NIGHTMARE

out of proportion was just fine with her, but then her expression softened.

"All right. Let's just get home."

"C'mon, C.J." Bob put a hand on his shoulder and led him off the beach, Susan and the girls following. As they departed, C.J. turned his head briefly to look back the way he had come.

He couldn't see the patch of beach where the man had been carrying the body from here, and there was no sign of him, either. That was good. Maybe he'd tell them all what he'd seen in the morning, when everyone had had a good night's sleep and Mom had had a chance to calm down.

\*\*\*

Further down the beach, George staggered out of the ocean and shivered. He pulled his trenchcoat tight around him, as if the sopping garment could offer any protection against the cold, and finally collapsed onto the sand. Panting from exertion, he looked up into the night sky. The rocket was gone, or perhaps its distant light was indistinguishable from the stars now.

The sudden eruption of fire and sound had overwhelmed him briefly; it shouldn't have come as such a surprise, considering how close he was to the Cape, but it had still been a shock to his system. Once it subsided, he had found a sudden strength and hauled the woman's corpse into the ocean, forcing his way through the water as far as he could go before releasing it. The rip currents were well known around here, and George figured they would take the body far enough, and hopefully out enough, that it would not be found for quite a while, if at all. Or maybe he'd be lucky and a shark would take it. Either way, he'd disposed of it now, and didn't have to worry about it anymore.

## MICHAEL GINGOLD

But now, as he lay there recovering physically, his mind began tilting again. Even in his exhaustion, he was afraid to close his eyes, because he knew that if he did he—

*—would be lying on the bed, bound and helpless, watching as the woman's head violently separated from her body and gouts of blood burst upward—*

He opened his eyes wide and cried out helplessly, but the vision could not be denied and—

*—now he was looking down at his father, who also screamed helplessly, first at the hideous act he had just witnessed, and then again as the weapon that committed it was raised over him . . .*

With another scream, now of defiance, George struggled to his feet. He jammed his hands into his pockets, but he already knew the pills weren't there; he had left them, the few he had remaining, on the bathroom counter in his motel room. And so he mentally fought back, trying to push the images away as—

*—more blood spurted forth, splattering onto the walls and the curtains and the dresser beside the bed, as he—*

"Enough!" he yelled, and focused on the scene around him. Not much to see, just darkened beach, with woods beyond. But beyond that was the car, and that could take him back to where he could lie down on the bed, and take the pills and hope they would, for just a little while, keep the awful sights away, and the urges that came with them.

If he could last that long.

\*\*\*

It was past midnight when the Cocoa Beach Theater 'n' Drafthouse let out the audience for its last show of the evening, a late screening of *Rock 'n' Roll High School*.

## NIGHTMARE

The crowd of teenagers and college-age kids was still buzzing from the movie, having enthusiastically taken in the saga of the Ramones battling the forces of authority.

A little too enthusiastically, for Sherry Gardner's taste.

Ordinarily, she loved going to movies at the Drafthouse. When it had first opened a couple of years ago, it seemed a little bit revolutionary, and Sherry and her friends loved the idea of a theater that served food beyond the usual popcorn and candy, even bringing it to your seat. Not to mention drinks beyond the usual Coca-Cola and Sprite. She was two months shy of her 18th birthday when the Drafthouse debuted, and she had counted the days until she was old enough to order a pitcher of beer to enjoy with the pizza or hot sandwich and whatever film she and her companions were taking in.

There had been many pitchers of beer tonight, one after another ordered by her boyfriend Gary and his friends Stu and Lester. Gary hadn't told Sherry that his buddies were joining them; she had hoped it would just be her and him together. Given her school schedule and his work schedule, they didn't get enough time to be with each other—not to mention that since they were both still living at home, the possibilities for getting it on were severely limited. Sex on the beach might sound exotic to some people, but when that was the setting more often than not, it made her yearn for coupling in the comfort of one of their beds.

She hadn't said anything, though, when she discovered they were going to be a foursome instead of a couple that night. And Stu and Lester weren't really bad guys. It was just that after not seeing Gary for days, the late-night show was the first thing this week that would absolutely not conflict with either of their commitments, and she had been looking forward to spending those two hours in the dark with him.

At least the movie had been good, and she loved the music. The problem was that so did Gary and Stu and Lester, and once they were a few pitchers in, they had taken to singing along with the songs onscreen. They weren't the only ones, and the audience participation didn't take her by surprise. It was a late-night movie, after all, and she had eagerly taken part in the call and response at a midnight screening of *The Rocky Horror Picture Show* a little while back. But she wanted to enjoy the Ramones' renditions and didn't feel like adding her own, and with the three guys happily contributing their increasingly drunken singalongs, clinking mugs at the end of each one, she felt increasingly left out the longer the movie went on. By the time it was over, Gary was so blitzed that she knew they couldn't have a coherent conversation about it. That would have to wait till their next date.

In the meantime, there was the more pressing question of getting home, since none of the trio were in any shape to drive. They didn't seem to think so, though, and once they hit the parking lot, they immediately started for their cars before Sherry stopped Gary with a hand on his shoulder.

"Gary, I really don't think you should drive right now."

"Why not? I'm fine."

He seemed a little more in control now than he had been in the theater, but she could still tell he was unsteady. "You've had too much to drink. You all have."

"No we haven't!" Lester chimed in, and Stu immediately replied, "Yes you have. You're half in the bag!"

# NIGHTMARE

"Well, if I'm half in the bag, you're half in the bag!"

"Oh yeah? Well, get out of my bag then, so I can get all in the bag!"

It was like a standup routine, and indeed, it wasn't the first time Sherry had heard it. She ignored them; right now, she wasn't as worried about how they got home, though she did hope nothing bad would happen to them. But Gary was her main concern.

"Just let me drive, okay?"

"Come on, Sherry, you know no one drives my car but me."

Shit. She had hoped that in his inebriated state, he would have forgotten about this rule, but no such luck. It was one of those silly rules that all guys seemed to have, and that they could not be dissuaded from. That had been the case with not one but two of her high-school friends, who had both been in accidents with drunken boyfriends. Thankfully, they had both walked away, though one had done so with a broken arm.

"Besides, your place is like a 10-minute drive from here."

"Ten minutes is all it can take, Gary. Just let me drive us there, and maybe my parents will let you crash."

"Yeah, sure. You know that ain't gonna happen."

He was very likely right, and that rather than her folks taking pity on his soused state and letting him sleep over on the couch, there would be disapproval and a major argument and who knows what else.

"Sherry, I promise, I'll get you home safe and—"

He took a step closer to her, to put a reassuring hand on her shoulder, and stumbled instead. She heard Lester snicker behind her, but paid him no mind.

"Gary, I'm sorry, I'm not getting in the car with you. Not in this state. Let's just call a cab."

"And leave my car here overnight?"

"Nothing's going to happen to it. It'll be perfectly safe."

"No way. My car goes where I go."

It was a weird statement to make, and she almost laughed. But nothing seemed very funny about this situation. The alcohol had made him stubborn, and she knew that the only way he was leaving here was behind the wheel. And she knew that she couldn't get in with him, even for the short ride to her place. She'd just have to call a cab for herself, and hope that he got back to his house safely.

No doubt he would, in fact, and tomorrow he would call her, safe and sound, and say she was chicken for not coming with him. She almost reconsidered, but she couldn't do it. She'd call a taxi herself, get back to the condo and hopefully sleep off the anger and frustration she was feeling right now.

"All right. I'm gonna get a cab. Just . . . drive carefully, okay?"

"I always do. You know that." He leaned in, gave her a beer-scented kiss, then spun around on his heel. "Onward, my good men!" he called, and Stu and Lester followed. "Good night!" they said in unison, with Stu throwing in, "Get home safe!"

"You too," she said as they headed off into the lot, and then went over to the pay phone at the corner of the theater building. She didn't have to look up the number; she'd used the local cab service enough to know it from memory.

Then she picked up the receiver and held it to her ear, and her heart sank. There was no dial tone.

"Damn it," she said, and tapped repeatedly on the

# NIGHTMARE

cutoff switch. She didn't know why; that had never worked the few times in the past when she'd encountered a dead phone, and it never worked for people on TV either. And it didn't work now.

"Damn it, damn it," she muttered, and walked quickly over to the theater entrance. She was pretty sure they had a phone in there she could use.

She reached the glass doors and peered in. The lights were dim now, and there didn't seem to be anyone inside. Which was strange, considering there was no doubt plenty of cleanup to be done. Maybe that's where everyone was, in the theater itself and not the lobby.

Rapping on the glass, she yelled, "Hello? Is someone in there? Hello, I need a phone!" She waited a minute, but no one emerged.

Stepping back a little, she looked over toward the lot. The last cars were starting to pull out, and she ran over, hoping maybe Gary's car would still be there. Maybe once he'd gotten in and sat down, he'd realized that he was not in fact in good shape to drive, and decided to wait and sleep it off a bit.

But no. His car wasn't in the spot where he'd parked, or anywhere else in sight.

"Oh, for God's sake!" Sherry said it loud, hoping maybe one of the last departing patrons would notice her and her predicament, and offer her a ride. She'd known better since childhood than to get into a car with a stranger, but this was becoming a desperate situation.

And as the last car turned out of the lot entrance and headed out down Brevard Avenue, something else occurred to her. The lot was completely empty now. If there was a cleanup crew in there, where were their cars? The whole thing didn't make sense.

Sherry had to resign herself to the fact that she was totally alone here. Now there was no other choice but to walk.

The prospect didn't frighten her as much as it annoyed her. Her place was indeed only a short drive away, but a short drive could equal a fairly long walk. Which she especially wasn't looking forward to this late at night.

Still, she realized that if she cut through parking lots, since it was mostly businesses between here and the condo, she could shave off some of the time. Then she further realized that though a lot of those businesses would be closed now, there was a motel about halfway home that would be open, and have a phone. She could call a cab from there, and give the driver a big tip, much bigger than he'd expect for such a short trip.

And so she set out, crossing Brevard and heading through the first lot across the way. It was a still night, and her footsteps sounded extra-loud to her as she made her way over the asphalt. She felt conspicuous, like the only person out there, and now she was a little scared. If anyone happened to be lurking out here . . .

She shook the thought away. She'd heard that walking confidently, like you really know where you're going and are not going to stopped, would send a signal to a potential attacker that you weren't to be messed with, and so she did her best to walk with more purpose, and a little faster, without breaking into a run.

Passing around the side of one building, she glanced quickly into the darkness behind it, just to be sure there wasn't some creep back there to threaten her. The space was empty, and she made her way across the adjacent lot with no problem. Then onto a

## NIGHTMARE

street, where there was more light, and she calmed down a little. This was going to be fine.

Sherry then thought, *Actually, I'm the one to be frightened of. I'm the one out here looking for victims.* She smirked, and realized that this was the real trick to handling a situation like this. Don't think of yourself as a potential victim, think of yourself as the bad guy, or girl, the one that other people should be afraid of. If there was anyone else out here wandering around after midnight, they should be scared to see her coming!

That thought got her down the street, across another wide, dark lot, and to the back of the lot behind the motel. She couldn't see the front from here, but she knew they'd be open, taking in lost travelers of the night. She made her way past the cars parked in the back of the lot, relieved that this little adventure would soon be over.

The attack happened so fast that she barely registered what was happening at first. From out of nowhere there was an arm around her waist and a hand over her mouth—a hand that smelled like the ocean—and she was being dragged backwards, past the cars and into the darkness at one side of the lot. She started to struggle, but whoever had hold of her was strong, stronger than she could resist.

She was thrown down, and her head hit something hard—a rock? A curb? It was hard to tell, it was all happening so fast. Dazed, she tried to sit up and scream, loud enough that someone in the motel that was so, so close would hear her . . .

Then that strong, salty hand was on her throat, pushing her back down. She saw a glint of metal in the air above her, and it swung down and her chest exploded in pain. For a few seconds it was all she could feel.

And then Sherry didn't feel anything at all anymore.

***

The dream was especially vivid. There hadn't been many where he was able to see and hear and feel so much, but this time the brightness and warmth of the sun, the sound of lapping water and wheeling, calling seagulls, and the uneven sand underfoot seemed so real. And to him, as he stirred in his bed and his subconscious took over, it was real.

He was back on the beach, the same part where he had been last night. But now it was daytime, not a cloud in the sky, and he thought briefly that it should be full of people enjoying the sun and the sea, but there was no one.

C.J. looked around, confused about being alone. That frightened him a little bit, and he had the feeling that there was something else scary here too, though he couldn't figure out what it was. It was like something bad had happened on this beach, something that had crawled back into the depths of his memory and wouldn't come out.

Part of him wanted to leave, and get back home. But . . . how? Neither his mom nor anyone else was with him, and with no other people or cars around, how would he get home? Here he was, out in the open, in the middle of the day, yet still he felt trapped.

He could only move toward the ocean, and so he did, in slow, halting steps, sensing that something awful was out there but he wasn't sure what, only that something was compelling him to see, to find out . . .

Then his foot hit something that made him stop, and he looked down. Even in the bright daylight, he couldn't quite make out what it was. It was just under the sand, and so he dropped to his knees and started digging.

# NIGHTMARE

Within seconds, he realized what the object was, and gasped. Yet he was compelled to keep uncovering it until it lay completely exposed.

It was a human hand—a man's hand, from the look of it. And something about that didn't seem right to C.J., as the dim thought occurred to him, *Wasn't that a woman's body that I* . . .

And before the thought was finished the hand rose up, not severed as he first thought but connected to an arm that emerged, sand spilling off it. Before C.J. could react, the hand grabbed the edge of his jacket and held on tight.

He tried to stand, but the grip was unbreakable, and then he tried to squirm out of his jacket but it was no use; somehow he couldn't shake it off. Looking around desperately, he still saw nobody, but he screamed anyway, and the wind off the ocean grabbed the sound and stole it away, carrying it off where it couldn't be heard.

Now something else was pushing up out of the sand behind the arm, and C.J. knew what it was going to be but screamed again anyway as a face emerged, and then the whole head. Its eyes bore into his, and fresh terror washed over C.J. as he realized who it was. It was the bad man, one he knew he had seen before but couldn't exactly remember where. All he knew was that he had to get away, somehow break free and get as far from the man as he could.

But it was impossible—the man's hold on him was too strong, and now it was pulling on him, drawing him closer. A look of anger spread over the man's face, and now C.J.'s was inches from him, and the man's other hand emerged from the sand and—

C.J.'s eyes flew open, his breath heaving and terrified, and for a few seconds he was confused.

Suddenly everything was dark, and he wasn't being dragged down onto rough sand but lying under the soft covers of his bed. It took his mind several seconds to adjust, and a little longer for him to get his breathing under control.

As he returned to his reality, the details of the nightmare began to slip from his mind. He was glad for that, but there was one thing that still clung to his memory: the face that had risen from the sand like a zombie in one of the movies C.J. liked to watch on TV. He'd been dreaming about the man he saw on the street, and on the beach.

It was bad enough that the man had scared him in real life, but now he was coming after C.J. in his dreams too. As he rolled over, pulling the covers up to his head and holding onto them tight, he thought it would be a while before he was able to get back to sleep.

# THE FOURTH DAY

**THE PHONE RANG**, and Dr. Williamson immediately picked it up. Whether it was good news or bad, he now wanted to hear it right away. This goddamn Tatum case was consuming his life right now, and however it was going to be resolved, he wanted it to just be over and done with. Maybe he'd lose his job, maybe not. But by this point, he'd resigned himself to hoping for the best and expecting the worst, as the song went.

It was still early, before his official office hours began, so he assumed it would be Jackson on the line, wanting to know if he'd heard any news of Tatum's whereabouts. Or, perhaps, even heard from Tatum himself. That was highly unlikely, of course; the man was in the wind, and the last thing he was going to do was call up for a chat. Hell, no one had even bothered to put a tap on Dr. Williamson's phone. He had thought at one point to suggest it, and then decided to keep silent. Let Jackson and the higher-ups make the decisions.

And so Dr. Williamson nearly fell off his chair when instead of Jackson's voice at the other end, he heard Tatum's.

"Doctor?" It was pained and unsteady, but definitely Tatum.

"George?" He switched the phone from one ear to the other, an odd habit he had when a call turned out to be more serious than expected. "George, is that you?"

"It happened again! Again!" He was almost crying, and Dr. Williamson felt his heart sink. He immediately knew what Tatum meant, and that everyone's worst fear about this case had been realized.

He thought to ask Tatum for details of what happened, but quickly realized they didn't matter. Only one thing did.

"All right, George, where are you?"

"It's stronger . . . stronger than the pills!" Then several seconds of silence from Tatum, during which Dr. Williamson strained to hear something, anything in the background that might offer the slightest clue as to where Tatum was calling from. "It takes me over!"

"George, I'm your friend. And it's important that you tell me where you are."

"It makes me do these things! Bad!"

"What makes you do those things?"

"The dreams! They won't go away, they won't stop! The pills can't make them stop, nothing can!"

If that was true, things were worse than they'd thought. Dr. Williamson had hoped that the meds could keep his behavior on an even keel until they could track him down, but now . . . now Tatum was evidently past that point, and who knew what he would do next?

"Listen to me, George. They're only dreams, and dreams can't hurt you!"

The next thing he heard was Tatum's scream in his ear, loud enough that he almost dropped the phone. There was a *thump* as if the phone had been dropped on something soft, and then another scream of anguish.

## NIGHTMARE

"Are you there, George?!" The answer was incoherent wailing, and sudden grunts like he'd been hit, though Dr. Williamson couldn't hear any sounds of him actually being struck.

"Daddyyyyyy!" It was a cry of complete, helpless agony, and Dr. Williamson almost felt sorry for him.

"George, don't hang up!" Now there was nothing but sobbing coming over the line, broken by gagging sounds. "George, get back on the line! Talk to me!"

But he didn't. The sobs softened into whimpers, and Dr. Williamson covered his free ear, trying again to discern any sort of sound revealing where Tatum was. And then he heard it—a distant but easily recognizable, high-pitched squeal. It was a seagull, and then came another, as if in response. He decided to give it one more try.

"George, please, tell me where you are so I can help you!"

He heard nothing in response. Even the birds fell silent. Then a *click* and the line was dead.

Dr. Williamson leaned back in his chair, the optimism he'd felt upon hearing the birds' calls starting to slip away. Okay, so Tatum was near the ocean. That didn't really help much. In theory, that meant he could be anywhere from Martha's Vineyard to Miami Beach, though as far as he knew from all their sessions, George had never been out of the five boroughs before. And there were plenty of possibilities there, from Coney Island to the Rockaways.

Should he tell Jackson about this? Dr. Williamson had to wonder if that would do any good. He'd gotten no solid information on where Tatum was, anything that could help track him down. The only things he'd learned from the call, if Tatum was to be believed, were that the meds weren't working now, and he'd claimed another victim. At least one—who knows how many? Tatum hadn't specified.

In other words, it was all bad, unhelpful news. As he considered it, Dr. Williamson realized that sharing this with Jackson wouldn't accomplish anything except getting him angrier. And Jackson was already plenty pissed as it was.

So there was only one other thing to make sure of. Tatum had his direct line, so he likely hadn't gone through the receptionist. And there was one way to find out.

He stepped out of the office and walked the short distance down the hall to Janice at the front desk. "I'm stepping out for a few minutes."

"Okay," she said. He thought perhaps she might have overheard his side of the conversation, as he had raised his voice pretty loud a couple of times; he'd have to be careful of that if it happened again. But Janice didn't give any indication of having heard anything.

And just to be absolutely positive . . . "Any calls for me this morning?"

"Nope. I would have put 'em through if there were."

"Thanks." He walked to the elevator and pushed the Down button. He didn't actually have anywhere to go, but a walk out in the crisp winter air would do him good. And when he got back, he'd call Jackson and ask if he'd heard anything on his end. Just to be sure.

\*\*\*

"Sounds like a nice location," Roger Burris said, and Susan had to agree. Their house was right across the street from Indian River, just like the Century 21 real estate office she was sitting in now.

"It is," she said, and gestured toward the windows. "In fact, if the bridge wasn't in the way, you might even be able see it from here."

# NIGHTMARE

"Well, my vision isn't what it used to be," he said with a chuckle, and Susan smiled. Though he seemed to be in his 50s, Roger was new to the agency, and he had a manner that immediately put Susan at ease. That helped a lot; if she was going to go through with selling the house and moving, it was going to be at least a little traumatic, and having someone friendly to steer the way would be a relief.

"How old's the house?" he asked.

"It must be over 50 years old, but it's in good shape." That was a bit of a lie, though if she could corral Bob and the kids to help straighten it up over the weekend, she could get it looking presentable.

"How many bedrooms?"

"Four bedrooms, ah, two baths, one upstairs, one downstairs. And it's got that beautiful view of the river."

"Sounds nice. I'd like to see the house. When can I come over?"

"You can come by sometime next week if you like."

"That sounds fine. In the meantime, I'll need some pictures, just like those on the wall there." She turned and looked over the instant photos arranged neatly on the wall behind her. "Just sample pictures. Polaroids will do." That would be easy enough; Bob had a Polaroid among his many other, more expensive cameras.

"Okay, I have a friend who can take them. I'll get them to you soon."

"Fine. I believe it'll sell. I believe it'll sell quickly. I want you to put your mind at ease, Mrs. Temper."

"Oh, it's Ms. And you can call me Susan."

"Well, all right, Susan. And if you're looking to relocate in the area, I can help you find a new place too."

"That would be great, thank you so much. You've been a lot of help."

"Thanks for coming in," he said with a smile.

It was such a pleasant meeting, Susan reflected as she left the office and walked to her car. After all the craziness with C.J., it was nice to have something go well, and smoothly. And who knows? Maybe getting out of that house really would be good for C.J. Even though he'd been way too young to experience or process the trauma around his father leaving them, perhaps he'd caught some kind of bad feelings that were only finding their way out now.

And maybe, just maybe, if they did find the right new house here on the Coast, Bob could be persuaded to move in and join them. Get him out of his damn boat, finally, and then they could all be a family.

Well, one thing at a time. Right now she had to go pick up him and his Polaroid so she could get this process started.

\*\*\*

George parked the car in the lot in front of the library, over in a far corner where it was less likely to be noticed, or for anyone to walk directly past it. Getting out, he walked casually to the side street and then to the main road along the water, turning to head up the sidewalk. He didn't hurry; no need to call attention to himself. He was just out for a stroll, as anyone might want to do on such a nice, sunny day.

He was calm now, the visions having eased away, sated by the killing of the girl last night. That was the only thing that placated his tortured mind now, the pills having lost their effect. After he had stabbed her—again and again, repeatedly, until the urges faded—his mind had become so clear, and disposing of her was easy. Only 20 yards or so away were a group of

## NIGHTMARE

dumpsters that looked like they hadn't been emptied in months. He had carried her over, making his way through darkness that hid his progress, and once he got close, the stink of rotting garbage was so rank that the smell of a decomposing body would barely be noticed. Opening the lid of one in the very back of the cluster, he hauled the corpse over the lip and in, where it landed not with a metallic *clong* but a wet rustling sound. Who knew what the hell else was putrefying in there.

Carefully closing the lid, he had made his way back to the motel, to his room, with absolutely no one around to see him. Taking off only his shoes, he had stepped into the shower with his clothes on, including the trenchcoat, and let the hot water wash the blood and the smell of the ocean down the drain. Then he'd hung the wet clothes up to dry, climbed into the bed naked, and slept the first undisturbed sleep he'd had in a while.

He knew it wouldn't last, though. It would likely be only a day or so before the visions would return, and he'd have to appease them again.

As he reached the house and turned up the side street, he thought that once he'd finished his business here, that might relieve him once and for all. He didn't know for sure, but it felt like the best possibility.

He walked more slowly down the side street, peering intently at the house. There was no noise or visible activity; it didn't seem like anyone was home. And that was good. Without hesitation, he turned off the street and walked around to the back of the house. Not hurrying, not looking around, but at a normal pace. Like he belonged there.

\*\*\*

## MICHAEL GINGOLD

A half hour later, Susan and Bob walked around the outside of the house, Bob snapping pictures with his Polaroid and dropping them into the little leather bag hanging from a strap over his shoulder. Susan laughed a little bit inside at how Bob treated what she considered a tourist camera as well as his much more expensive ones. He had in fact offered to bring one of his Nikons out for this little shoot, but she assured him it wouldn't be necessary. She needed the pictures fast and easy, not artistic.

Still, he didn't let it go. As they reached the front of the house and he readied to snap a photo there, he said, "You know, asking me to take a Polaroid is sort of like asking Picasso to paint your car."

"You might as well make your car a work of art. You never drive it."

"I drive it plenty!"

"Only when I'm not around to drive you," she smiled. He smiled back, and raised the camera. "Say cheese," he said, and *click*, another picture slid out of the Polaroid.

"Mind if I see them?"

"Not at all," Bob said, taking the other photos out of the bag and handing them to her. She took them over to the front steps, sat down, and went through them while Bob waited for the new one to develop.

As the house faded up into view, Bob noticed something in one of the upstairs windows. It was hard to tell in such a small snapshot, but it looked like . . .

"Hey, come here." She got up and joined him. "There's nobody in the house, is there?"

"No, the kids are still at school."

"Well, take a look at this."

He handed her the photo, and it took her a few

moments to realize what he was talking about. But once she saw it, she let out a small gasp.

There was someone visible in one of the upstairs windows. She couldn't make out the details, but he was clearly there.

"Is that a man there? What's going on?"

She held the picture up to get a better look, then joined Bob in looking up at that window, where there was nothing but a dark room behind the glass.

"There's no one there now," Bob said. "Let's take a look."

Susan hesitated at first; what if someone was inside? Shouldn't they find a phone and call the police? But Bob was already running for the side door, and she didn't want him going in alone.

She caught up to him as he entered the house, and together they walked in, stopping a few steps past the door.

"Who's in there?" she called out. When there was no answer, Bob said quietly, "Let's go upstairs."

She went to follow him, then darted into the kitchen, pulled open a drawer and grabbed the biggest knife she could find. They made their way up the stairs and down the hallway slowly, Bob gently pushing open the door to the room where they had seen the figure in the photo.

Finding no one inside, Bob turned to Susan—and jumped when he saw the knife in her hand. "What are you doing with that?"

"Just in case."

"Well, be careful with it."

They went to the other bedrooms, and the bathroom. All were empty, and Susan relaxed, putting the knife down on a little table in the hallway.

"There sure isn't anything up here now," Bob said.

"It's so strange."

"Maybe our imaginations are getting affected by C.J.'s."

She was still holding the photo, and she raised it again. "I believe what I see here."

"Hey, it's probably nothing. There's probably a very simple explanation."

"Like what? Bob, a lot of strange things are happening in this house."

"This is instant film. And a cheap camera. It's probably just a light leak, or a shadow on the emulsion."

He gently took the picture from her. "Did you ever see that Antonioni film *Blow-Up*?" She shook her head, and he continued, "This guy thinks he sees a murder in a photograph, and he keeps blowing it up bigger and bigger and bigger, trying to see the murder."

"Yes, okay, there was nothing in that picture. Give it to me, let me see it again."

He did, and she gave it another look, and maybe he was right. The figure wasn't that distinct, after all.

"So there was no murder in that movie?"

"Oh yeah, there was. There was a murder."

His expression was dead serious for a few seconds before he broke into a big smile.

"Thanks a lot," she laughed. "That's very reassuring."

"Come here."

He embraced her, rubbing her back. "Don't worry. Everything's fine." She looked into his eyes, and right then she believed him. His lips met hers—

—and George, watching from a closet, tensed up. He could feel the visions creeping back, about to spring into his mind, triggered by the sight of the two of them kissing. His grip tightened on the knife he held in one hand, the other holding the door, tensing, ready to push it fully open and leap out. They had been lucky they hadn't checked the closet, but if they kept up the way they were, he wouldn't be able to control himself much longer.

And just as that thought passed through his mind, they separated.

"Tell you what," Bob said. "Let's pick the kids up after school and go to the beach."

"I like that idea," Susan replied, and they walked back down the hallway.

George couldn't see them now, but heard their footsteps down the stairs, followed shortly by a door opening and closing. A short wait, and then the sound of a car starting and pulling away.

He relaxed, just a little, and stepped out of the closet. After standing in silence briefly, he too headed for the stairs. He didn't hurry, because he didn't need to. He knew where they were going.

\*\*\*

Jackson sat at the monitor, four faces of George Tatum once again gazing at him from around the main screen. And this time, he had actual human company in the room with him, too. Daniels, Cooper's latest lapdog, sent down to oversee Jackson's progress.

Actually, Jackson had to admit, this guy seemed a lot smarter and more competent than the other underlings he'd dealt with. Daniels had only been with Cooper's division for a few months, so Cooper's arrogance hadn't had sufficient time to rub off, Jackson surmised. He wouldn't say what area of the government he had worked for before Cooper brought him on, but clearly it had something to do with computer science, because he had given Jackson access to programs that could gather intelligence in a way Jackson had never seen or heard of before.

As Jackson tapped at the keyboard, Daniels pored through one of Tatum's files, and whistled softly. "Damn. You really believed someone who would do this could be cured?"

He was looking at photos of the Brooklyn family, and seemed not repulsed but curious that one human being could do that to others.

"Believe it or not, we've seen people who have done worse," Jackson said, not taking his eyes off the screen.

"Have you cured any of them?"

"A couple. Some can be reached and some can't. You never know till you try."

That seemed to satisfy Daniels, who flipped further through the file as Jackson finished typing and text began to scroll up the monitor.

**CODE: EYES ONLY**
**QUERY:**
**RESULTS**
**ALL POINTS BULLETIN**
**SUBJECT: TATUM**

Jackson typed some more, followed by:

**RE: APB 626-4**
**TATUM VEHICLE**
**BR. FORD MAVERICK**
**N.Y. LIC. #605-GLM**
**FOUND:**
**MYRTLE BEACH, SOUTH CAROLINA**

"Found Myrtle Beach?" Jackson pondered. "What the hell is he doing in South Carolina?"

# NIGHTMARE

**SUSPECT:**
**WHEREABOUTS NOT KNOWN**
**LOCAL POLICE REFERENCE #**
**1874-SCSP-16**

"Well, he's sure as hell not a walker. Let's see if he stole another car."

Daniels closed the file and put it aside, watching as Jackson typed further, clearly marveling at the information now literally at his fingertips.

**QUERY:**
**SCAN LOCAL MISSING VEHICLE**
**REPORTS—24 HOUR PERIOD AFTER**
**DISCOVERY OF TATUM VEHICLE**

Jackson punched another button, and stared intently at the screen as the results scrolled up.

**MISSING VEHICLE REPORTS—LOCAL:**
**79 GRN/WHT OLDS**
**S.C. LIC. PLATE**
**# 31879-N**
**OWNER MISSING**
**PRESUMED DEAD**

"Oh, shit," Jackson sighed. Suddenly he wasn't happy at all to have this access; now he hoped he could pull up enough results to quickly stop what was shaping up to be another bloodbath.

**OWNER:**
**BARBARA STOCKTON**
**FEM. CAUC. AGE 26**

## MICHAEL GINGOLD

**LAST SEEN:
GATSBY'S RESTAURANT
MYRTLE BEACH, SC**

Jackson took the cigar out of his mouth, and let out a long, smoky breath. Daniels raised a hand, waving it a couple of times to dispel the smoke. It was a gesture Jackson disliked from most people, but he'd let this one go. He typed some more:

**QUERY:
WHY PRESUMED DEAD?**

He pushed the button and got his answer:

**SUBJECT'S APT CONTAINS MASSIVE
BLOOD STAINS ON FLOORS AND WALLS
BLOOD TYPE MATCHES SUBJECT
NO BODY FOUND
NO SUSPECTS**

Daniels let out another low whistle, and Jackson muttered, "Oh boy" as he typed once more.

**QUERY:
CROSS REFERENCE AND COLLATE
ALL KNOWN DATA ON TATUM:
PREDICT DESTINATION
POSSIBILITIES**

This time, it took a little longer for the computer to respond. "Come on, come on!" Jackson said, and then he had to laugh on the inside. Ten minutes with this program that was feeding him intel that would otherwise require hours of phone calls and waiting to gather, and he was already getting impatient with it.

**PROBABLE DESTINATIONS:**
**BRADEN SC ... 19%**
**ATLANTA GA ... 31%**
**MIAMI FL ... 63%**
**DAYTONA FL ... 91%**

"Daytona?" Jackson marveled. He didn't think he'd get a result with that percentage of certainty. "Daytona Beach?"

"Ever been?" Daniels asked.

"Not yet. But I guess I'm going now."

"We're going." Jackson looked over at him. Daniels was smiling a little, but clearly not kidding.

"OK, I guess we're going to go down there and find him now."

\*\*\*

The screaming of the seagulls over Susan was becoming deafening, and their shadows made the sunlight flicker in her eyes, and she'd had enough. "C.J., could you get those damn birds out of here!"

C.J., who was feeding the gulls out of a plastic bag, turned and ran from the little picnic spot they'd set up on a quiet part of the beach. The birds followed, but not fast enough for Susan. "Look at 'em! Look at 'em! They're all over the damn place."

She lay back down beside Bob, who was going to observe that this was to be expected since they were by the water, then decided against it. Instead, he watched as C.J. continued to run, throwing the last of the leftovers to the hungry gulls. "See? They're going now."

"Good. The last thing I want is them pooping on me when I'm trying to relax."

Tammy and Kim, who were digging in the sand and hadn't seemed to notice the birds one way or the other, both giggled at that.

"Well, maybe they'll poop on C.J. now instead," Bob said. The girls giggled at that too, and even Susan smiled. That was better, and he took her hand in his. "Let's just enjoy the day, okay?"

"Okay."

Then it was just the sounds of the ocean and the wind, and the birds—much better now that they were distant—and it was calm. With any luck, C.J. would find ways to amuse himself for a while. He had the binoculars, so maybe he would go scope out Cape Canaveral. As long as he didn't go too far . . .

C.J., meanwhile, a ways up the beach, was indeed using the binoculars to check out the Cape. And wondering how far he could and should go. Neither Mom nor Bob had told him to stay close, so he thought he could walk quite a long way, as long as he got back to them before the sun started to go down.

He lowered the binoculars to run, and only made it a short distance further before he saw the person standing, looking out over the water. C.J. stopped, suddenly nervous. Even though he was pretty far away, he knew with a terrible certainty who it was.

And when he looked through the binoculars again, that fear was confirmed. The man in the trenchcoat turned and looked . . . at him, or just in his general direction? It was hard to tell, and if the man had spotted him, he didn't react. He looked back out at the ocean—and then back toward C.J. Right at him this time, C.J. was sure of it.

His heart beating so loud he thought maybe the man could hear it, C.J. turned and dashed back toward his family. It seemed like it took forever to reach them,

# NIGHTMARE

and none of them seemed to hear as he yelled, "Mom! Mom!", the wind carrying the words away.

Finally he was back, and they could hear him now, Tammy falling aside in surprise as C.J. ran up to Susan. He slipped and fell to the sand, then looked up with panic in his eyes.

"Mom! That man's down the beach! The man that's been following me!"

He sat up, his breathing heavy and scared. He could tell right away that his mom was more angry than concerned, and even Bob seemed annoyed.

"C.J., have you heard the story of the boy who cried wolf?" Bob asked.

"I'm not lying! He's right down there!"

He pointed back the way he came, but Susan wasn't having it. She leaned in, grabbed him roughly by the shoulders and shook him.

"That's enough! I've had it with you, and I've had it with these stories!"

"Relax," Bob said. "Will you just relax?"

C.J. knew there was no use trying to convince them, and so he got up and ran off, away from them, away from the man, away from everyone. Susan yelled after him, "Sure, C.J.! What did you see, a man from Mars down there? No more stories, C.J.! I've had it!"

"Relax, relax!" Bob said again, standing. "I'll go talk to him."

"If you think it'll do any good."

"I think it might do better than screaming at him."

"I've just, I've had enough, Bob. He just won't stop."

"Let me see if I can get through to him."

"I hope you can. Good luck."

Bob headed off in C.J.'s direction, wondering if he could in fact reach C.J., and get him to stop with the tricks and the fantasies. He knew that Susan was at the end of her rope, and he couldn't blame her, but he had always believed in the idea that there was a solution to everything, and perhaps he had it here.

He found C.J. sitting behind a patch of tall grass, picking absently at the sand in front of him. He didn't look up as Bob sat down beside him.

"Hey, partner."

"I'm not lying!" C.J. said right away, and the look on his face almost convinced Bob that he wasn't.

"Nobody says you're lying."

"Mom is."

"Well, after what you pulled the other day, can you blame her?"

"Okay, that was a joke. But I'm not lying now. I saw him down the beach, and he was at the house, he really was! And . . . "

"And what, C.J.?"

"If I tell you something, promise you won't tell Mom?"

Bob considered that a moment. He knew he shouldn't keep secrets from Susan where her kids were concerned. But C.J. looked genuinely scared, and Bob decided that he should know why, and that telling someone might make the boy less frightened.

"Okay. I promise."

"Last night, when I went down the beach? I saw him then too. And he had a dead body with him!"

"What?"

"I swear. He was carrying a dead person, I think he was going to throw them into the ocean."

"Are you sure that's what you saw? It was so dark . . . "

"Positive! When the rocket went off, it lit up the beach and then I could see. He had a dead body!"

His eyes were wide, and Bob could tell C.J. truly

# NIGHTMARE

believed that's what he saw. Or was it just a performance? Just part of an act? After all, C.J. had had them pretty convinced he'd been stabbed and in pain the other day. And it was one thing to say somebody was following him, but now bringing murder into the mix . . .

C.J.'s expression turned to disappointment, and Bob could tell the boy saw the doubt in his eyes.

"You don't believe me, do you?"

"I wish I could believe you for sure, C.J. But you do tell a mean story. You know, you're getting a reputation as the Cocoa Pinocchio."

The joke didn't work at all, and C.J. just dropped his gaze to the sand.

"Look, these things are just stories to you, but you know, you really upset your mother. It's hard on her, you know? You're getting older, you're kind of the man of the house now, and you've got to take care of her. You understand?"

"I guess."

He didn't look up, and Bob decided to try a different tack.

"So you say this man who's after you was just there now?"

C.J. perked right up. "Swear on a stack of Bibles!"

"Okay. Let me take a look."

He lifted the binoculars on their strap from around C.J.'s neck, stood up and surveyed the beach with them. It seemed deserted . . . except, yes, there was somebody out there, so far that it was hard to make them out even with the binoculars.

"That guy down there, walking all by himself? Is that the guy you saw?"

C.J. stood and Bob handed him the binoculars. After gazing through them, he said softly, "I don't know. I'm not sure."

## MICHAEL GINGOLD

"C.J. . . ."

"You see? Nobody believes me."

Bob was at a loss now. He couldn't believe C.J. about this, not when he kept embellishing and then holding back this way, but clearly something was troubling him, some reason he was persisting with this story. If only he could—

"Do you like my mom?" The question startled Bob. For all the months he'd been dating Susan, and the time spent with C.J., the boy had never expressed any curiosity about their relationship.

"I like your mom very much."

"You think you might marry her?" That took Bob equally by surprise. Of course he did, but the answer wasn't that simple.

"What made you ask that?"

"Mmm, I'm just curious."

Bob considered his reply carefully, and decided it would be best to make it another question. "How would you feel about that?"

"I'd feel great! And then you'd be my father and you'd live with us, right?"

Now at least part of the reason for what had been going on dawned on Bob, but he didn't feel now was the right time to pursue it with C.J. He'd definitely discuss it with Susan soon, though.

"You know what, C.J.?"

"What?"

"I'd be very proud to be your father."

"So you are going to marry her!"

Bob smiled. "Let's not get ahead of ourselves here. That's a big decision. It's not something you just jump into."

"You love her, right?"

"I do."

# NIGHTMARE

"Then why not?"

"C.J., it's . . . There are things you're just too young to understand." It was a cop-out answer, but the necessary one right now. "But believe me, I am thinking about it."

"Okay. But I hope you decide soon."

"C.J., you'll be the first—well, second one to know when I do."

"Okay." That seemed to placate him.

"And, C.J.?"

"Yeah?"

"I'll keep your secret, but you have to keep what we just talked about secret, all right?"

"All right."

"Good. Now let's go back to your mom. And no more talk about that man now. Promise?"

"Promise."

Bob took C.J.'s hand, and they started back toward Susan. There was peace now, and Bob hoped it would last.

\*\*\*

"Why do you have to go out *again*?" C.J. cried as Susan put on her jacket, Kathy took off her sweater and Bob waited in the sitting room.

"It's just for a couple of hours," Susan said. "We're just going to dinner, we won't be out too late."

"Why don't you just have dinner here? Bob can stay and we'll all have it together."

"C.J., we were together all afternoon. Bob and I just want a little time to ourselves, okay? Kathy can get dinner for you."

"I don't want Kathy to get dinner!"

Kathy looked at Susan quickly and then retreated back into the living room. She knew better than to get involved.

"Why can't we all go out together?" C.J. persisted.

"We'll go out together another night."

"Tomorrow?"

"Maybe. We'll see. We'll talk about that tomorrow, okay?"

"Fine." C.J. stalked over to and up the stairs, followed by the sound of a slamming door.

Susan looked over to Kathy. "I'm sorry about that."

"Maybe if I'm lucky, he'll stay in there all night."

"Just make sure he eats something, okay?"

"I will. You and Bob have a good time."

"Thanks." Bob came out of the sitting room and joined Susan as she opened the door. "See you later."

*Not too much later*, Kathy thought. She hoped they didn't decide to head out for drinks after dinner and make it a longer night. This had been a last-minute call from Susan, and the moment she had stepped in the door, Kathy could tell C.J. wasn't happy about it.

Well, let him sit up there all night and sulk. She would wait till later, and then make one, just one, offer to get him some dinner. If he turned her down, she wasn't going to push it. Let him go hungry, if that's what he wanted. At least then he wouldn't have the energy to go climbing around on the roof. Never mind whatever prank he might try to pull from up there; if he wasn't careful, the little brat might slip and fall and break his neck, and then it would no doubt be her fault.

Still, since the first time he'd done something like that, she'd occasionally caught herself wishing he would do just that. Not kill himself in the process, but get banged up enough that he would learn his lesson. Every so often, at odd moments, she caught herself imagining C.J. taking that plunge, like a sight gag out of a *Pink Panther* movie. She pictured herself lounging in front of the TV and hearing a funny sound from above her, and then seeing C.J. drop past the window to land with a *thud* on the unseen ground outside. It made her giggle whenever she thought about it.

Fortunately, the night passed without incident. Kathy helped Kim with her math homework, using those silly flash cards she remembered from when she was in elementary school. Then she ordered a pizza, and for the first and only time, she went upstairs and knocked on C.J.'s door.

"C.J.? I ordered a pizza, come on down in 15 minutes if you want some!"

A faint rustling came from inside, as if C.J. was shifting around on his bed. Or maybe, knowing him, trying to hide something. She wasn't about to go in to investigate, though; the less contact she had with him, the better. "C.J.?"

"I'm not hungry," came the disinterested reply.

"Okay. Let me know if you change your mind."

And that was that. She went back downstairs, and she and the girls had enjoyed their pizza dinner. Tammy and Kim were a little upset that she hadn't ordered soda to go with it, but she didn't need them bouncing off the walls just before bedtime.

Instead, she had seen them peacefully to bed, and on the way back down the hall, she stopped outside C.J.'s door. Cupping her hand against it, she leaned in and listened for any sign of life, but there was only silence. She was about to move on when it occurred to her that he could have sneaked out somehow, through a window or even the door while she was distracted downstairs, and decided she had to be sure.

Slowly turning the knob, she opened the door just enough to let a sliver of the hallway light fall across the bed. The room was otherwise dark, and C.J. lay under the covers, fast asleep.

Relieved, Kathy quietly closed the door and made her way back downstairs. That was good. It would be a peaceful night for once, and—

She was right beside the phone when it rang, making her jump. She quickly grabbed the receiver off its cradle, hoping it hadn't awakened C.J.

"Hello?"

The voice was low and growly, and static crackled on the line as it spoke. "I want you. I want you so badly."

"Joey? Is that you?" She'd had to break her date with him tonight to take this job, but she needed the money. "Come on, you can do better than that."

Only more static answered her. "Joey? Are you there?"

More static, and then the line went dead. She looked at the phone curiously, then hung it up. She'd actually hoped Joey would continue, and they could have a fun little conversation while the kids were sleeping. But apparently not. No action of any kind tonight.

Kathy checked her watch, and saw that it would be about half an hour before Susan returned. She could watch some TV, or call up one of her girlfriends and see what they were up to. Then she decided that what she really wanted was a nice long shower.

Minutes later, she was standing under the water, letting its heat wash over her as the room filled with steam. With the kids all in bed, she could spend a little time in here, letting all the tension drain away. For once, it would be an uneventful night.

She finished shampooing, running her fingers through her long blonde hair till it was squeaky clean.

## NIGHTMARE

Then she began soaping herself, and as she ran her hands over her body, she thought about Joey. She knew he was a little upset about her cancelling on him, but she also knew that she'd make it up to him sometime soon. And as for right now, well, as she ran her hands over her breasts, slippery from the soap, she figured she could take care of herself as she touched herself more softly and—

*Nope, nope.* Not here. Not with three little kids in rooms just a few feet down the hall. Even though they wouldn't know what was going on, it wasn't right.

She finished showering, wrapped a towel around herself and made sure it would stay put before opening the bathroom door to let the steam disperse. A quick look out into the hall confirmed that no one was there, and she grabbed another towel and wrapped it around her hair. Sliding open the mirrored door of the medicine cabinet, she took out a bottle of lotion and quickly rubbed a little onto her hands, then replaced the bottle and slid the cabinet door closed.

A horrible face leered back at her from the mirror, red eyes burning in the darkness of the doorway, the hallway light catching its bald head. She screamed as it loomed closer to her, then again as she pushed past it and fled down the stairs.

Kathy stopped in the living room, catching her breath, recovering from her fright. As she composed herself and her mind cleared, she realized there was nothing to be scared of at all. She understood what had just happened, and her momentary terror quickly subsumed into rage.

And just to confirm that realization, and add one final insult to it, C.J.'s voice taunted down from upstairs: "Nanny nanny boo-boo, stick your head in doo-doo!" Followed by a raspberry. It made Kathy want to get a knife from the kitchen, go up there and cut his tongue out.

\*\*\*

Susan had in fact returned home only 10 minutes or so later, and Kathy had just enough time to get dressed before she came in the front door. C.J., of course, had run into his room with his oversized black costume and rubber full-head mask and locked the door. Kathy knew she wouldn't be able to cajole or threaten him out, but she was going to give Susan a piece of her mind when she got back.

And so she did, explaining what had happened and letting Susan know she was done. "I can't babysit anymore, I can't take it anymore. I just can't!"

Before Susan could respond, she went for the door and got out as far as the top of the driveway before Susan caught up with her.

"Wait a minute now, just wait," Susan said, grabbing Kathy's wrist. She held on just tight enough that Kathy couldn't pull away easily, so instead she whirled and got right in Susan's face.

"C.J. is not normal! He is evil, there's something bad inside him!"

Susan released her wrist, and for a second, Kathy saw something in her eyes that said she understood, that she had gone through some of the same problems. It was gone quickly, though.

"He just likes to play games, you know that," Susan said. "I'll have him call you later and apologize."

"Yeah, and I'm sure he'll mean it. And then the same thing will happen next time."

"Trust me, I'll see to it that it does not happen again."

"You can't change him! He is scary! He scares you, he scares me, he scares everybody! I just can't take it anymore!"

# NIGHTMARE

Kathy stormed down the driveway, and Susan ran up behind her, putting an arm around her. It was a gesture she did not appreciate.

"Come on, Kathy, calm down . . ."

"No!" she shouted, shaking Susan off. "He's just getting worse, and I'm at the point where I'm ready to kill him if he does it again."

"How can you say that about a nine-year-old child?"

"Not a normal nine-year-old child. I don't know how you deal with him, but I don't have to anymore, and I won't."

"Kathy, I need you!"

"Why, because no one else will babysit him? Well, you'll have to find someone, because I'm finished. I may need the money, but . . . no!"

"Kathy, please!"

She ignored Susan and walked out onto the street. As she went, she caught C.J. in the corner of her eye, watching her from his bedroom window. She turned to face him—and immediately regretted it. She shouldn't have acknowledged him at all.

He pulled the curtains shut, and Kathy continued off to the main road. It would be the last time she made this walk, and she just prayed she found some other job—any other job—quickly.

Up in his room, C.J. lay down on his bed, waiting for his mom to come knocking at his door. He'd be in trouble again, but it was worth it for the look on Kathy's face when she'd seen the mask he'd wired up with red lights in its eyes. The little battery pack Tony had lent him worked perfectly, and he had given Kathy her biggest scare yet. And from what he had heard of their shouted conversation outside, it seemed this one had done the trick.

## MICHAEL GINGOLD

He heard footsteps coming up the stairs, and got ready to be scolded, or whatever punishment Mom had in store for him. Instead, there was the sound of her bedroom door opening and closing, and then silence.

So she wasn't going to yell at him tonight. That was good—unless she was taking some extra time to think up a new way to punish him. That wouldn't be so good. But there was nothing he could do about it. He'd just have to get to sleep and find out what was going to happen in the morning.

Down the hall, lying in her own bed, Susan was not in fact thinking about punishment. The situation was beyond that now. Kathy was right—not about the evil part, but that there didn't seem to be anything she could do to solve his behavior. She was going to have to find help from others now, and put him in the hands of people who had more experience with this sort of thing.

*Jesus, sending a nine-year-old to a shrink.* It seemed almost unimaginable, but Susan knew it happened. But it happened to other people's kids, children who had real mental problems, not little boys who were just acting out. It was just a phase they grew out of.

Yet Susan knew that more was going on with C.J. She'd known it for a little while now, and she was finally resigning herself to what she had to do about it. She'd make some calls next week.

Just as she had that thought, the phone rang. It made her smile, for the first time since she'd gotten home. Maybe someone had read her thoughts and was getting in touch with her! If only. It was probably Bob, just calling to say good night. Or—damn—it could be Kathy's parents, in a mood to berate her for C.J. scaring their daughter. She'd never heard from them before, but given the mood Kathy was in when she left ... And she realized that in the heat of those moments, she hadn't paid Kathy.

All those thoughts ran through Susan's head in a couple of seconds, before she picked up the phone to find out for sure. "Hello?"

It sounded like a bad connection, or a cheap phone on the other end. But the voice was more than clear enough.

"I want you. Oh my God, I want you so bad."

For a second, she thought it was Bob, in a randy frame of mind. As quickly as the possibility occurred to her, she knew it wasn't. It didn't sound at all like him.

"I know you. I've ... seen you."

"Who is this?" Kathy's boyfriend, getting a bit of revenge? It could be, and better that than some perverted stranger.

"I saw your body, your legs. I want to touch them. All over ... "

"Stop it!"

"To be in your bed, my body over yours. Feeling you, feeling your skin ... "

"Listen, I'm going to call the police if you don't stop this!"

"I know you're alone, and I'm coming ... "

She decided on a different tack. If it was some stranger, how would he know who was there?

"I'm not alone. My husband's here, and he has a gun and if he finds out who you are—"

"There's no husband there. No man is there with you. Not yet ... "

"Yes there is, and he'll get you if the police don't. Don't you call here again!"

She slammed the phone down and watched it,

steeling herself for the inevitable ring when the creep called back. But it remained silent, and after a few minutes, she relaxed. Picking up a cigarette box lying beside the phone, she extracted one, lit it and lay back. Now it was obscene phone calls too. As if she didn't have enough insanity in her life right now.

# THE FIFTH DAY

**C****ANDY BENEDICT LEFT** her house and jogged the short distance down to the river road, then began her run along the water. It was a perfect day for it, sunny and pleasant and not too hot. During the summer, she would sometimes come back from her runs feeling sweaty and gross, and she wished the weather could be like it was in the winter year-round.

She often considered moving somewhere north, maybe Maryland, where her older brother lived. But that would have to wait. She had started her job at the hotel six months ago, and it was a good one—aside from having to duck the occasional advances from Walter, the assistant general manager—with strong possibilities for moving up, and she didn't want to leave that. She had also found a good, affordable couple of rooms in a house with a landlord she really liked, and she didn't want to leave that either. So Cocoa Beach would be her home for the foreseeable future, and there were certainly worse places to live.

As she continued up the road, she heard the clicking of bicycle wheels behind her, and C.J. rode up on his 10-speed, keeping pace with her. "Hi, Candy!" he said brightly.

"Hey, C.J.! What are you up to today."

"I'm going to feed my birds."

## MICHAEL GINGOLD

"Your birds? Where?"

"Just down the road a little."

"Okay. You staying out of trouble?"

"Yep!"

"You sure?"

"Positive! I'll see you around."

He picked up speed and headed off down the road. Watching him go, Candy wondered just how honest he had been. Her younger brother was friends with Kathy Morrison, and apparently C.J. had been giving her quite a bit of trouble lately. Which surprised Candy, because when she had babysat C.J. a few years back, he hadn't acted any worse than any other kid his age. Maybe there was something going on at home. Anyway, it wasn't her concern, and her thoughts turned elsewhere as she continued her jog.

Up ahead, C.J. saw Tony coming towards him on his own bicycle, and hopped off his. Tony just had a one-speed, and C.J. teased him once in a while about it, but then Tony's dad was in electronics and sometimes gifted him with the latest gadgets, so C.J. couldn't make too much fun of him there.

"Hey, C.J., how come you're over here?" Tony asked as he stopped.

"Oh, I'm just hanging around. I'm gonna feed the birds. Wanna help?"

"Sure! Oh wait, I've got to go to my house first, but I'll be back."

"Okay, I'll see you later!"

They biked off in opposite directions, and Tony soon passed Candy, giving her a wave. She waved back and jogged on.

Ten minutes later, she slowed her pace as she approached the old, abandoned house sitting at the water's edge; that was her landmark, where she would

# NIGHTMARE

turn around and head back home. As she got closer, though, she saw something that stopped her.

It was a bicycle, leaning up against the house by the front door. She walked over and gave it a closer look, and recognized it as C.J.'s.

That wasn't right; kids shouldn't be hanging around in this crumbling old place. It had been sitting unoccupied as far back as she could remember, and time and weather had stripped almost all the paint off the outside walls. Inside, it was likely at least some of the floors had started rotting away. Even though Candy and her friends had explored it a few times when they were younger, she knew better now.

She opened the front door and peered inside. "C.J.? C.J., are you in here?"

When she got only silence in return, she hesitated for a moment. Of course he was in there, if his bike was here, and maybe he was somewhere inside preparing one of the pranks she had heard he had pulled on Kathy. Still, there was also a good chance he was upstairs and just couldn't hear her, and she felt a strong need to get him out of there before he got hurt.

Entering the house, she started up the stairs, relieved to find they were still solid. "C.J.? C.J.?" she called out as she reached the second floor.

It was dark up here, with only a couple of bands of sunlight piercing through the windows of the rooms off the hallway. She made her way more tentatively down to the other end, looking into each room as passed it, seeing nothing but broken, rusting furniture and junk strewn across the floors.

She took a few steps into what had once been a bedroom, where a bunk bed stood with its stained mattresses collapsed to the bottom of the frame. Something rustled near her feet, and she looked down to see a large black rat emerge with a squeak from under a couple of old magazines.

Candy jumped back into the hallway, letting out a little startled shriek. Now she was getting annoyed. "C.J., are you up here?"

Still nothing, and she opened the door at the end of the hall and stepped into the room beyond. This one was better lit, sun streaming in through the large windows facing the river, but all Candy could see was more dilapidated furnishings and more trash, plus a number of empty liquor bottles—evidence of other recent visitors.

"Damn it, C.J.!" She was sure at this point that he was at the very least hiding, if not plotting something more. She was about to leave when she noticed something through one of the windows, and went over to get a better look outside.

There was C.J., standing midway down a long, narrow pier stretching across the water from the back of the house, feeding seagulls from a plastic bag. Candy was relieved; the pier didn't look completely stable either, but it was certainly a safer place to be than the house. And now she could get the hell out of here too.

She turned to go, and let out another little shriek. A man was standing partially behind the opened door to the hallway, staring at her.

Had he been there the whole time? Obviously he had, and the idea that he had been watching her freaked Candy out even more.

He closed his eyes and shook his head quickly and violently, and to Candy it looked like he was trying to get a bad thought out of his head. When his eyes opened again, they stared at her in a way that made her heart stop.

She looked around for something she could use to

# NIGHTMARE

defend herself, but in seconds he was upon her, grabbing her and dragging her across the room. She only got out one brief scream before he slammed her against the door, so hard she heard wood snap.

Then he brought up a knife, and her mind barely acknowledged it before she felt fire burn across her throat. She saw blood spatter onto his face, and it took her a disbelieving second to realize it was her own.

Candy tried to scream, but no sound would come, and the man let her go but she couldn't walk anymore, and she collapsed to the floor. She saw more of her own blood pool and spurt across the discolored wood, and she had just a moment to wonder why and how this was happening to her, and then the whole world went dark.

\*\*\*

Tony walked past C.J.'s bicycle, and the NO TRESPASSING sign on the wall, to the front door of the house. He didn't really like hanging out here; his parents had told him not to, and he had to admit it kind of scared him, but he'd only admit that to himself. C.J. was braver than he was, and Tony never wanted to look like a chicken.

He went inside and looked around. "C.J., are you in here?" He said it quietly, as if someone other than C.J. might hear him, and then felt silly, because who else would be here? Other than older kids hanging out and smoking and drinking, and they only came late at night, as far as Tony knew.

With no sign of C.J. down here, Tony went to the stairs and started up. He almost wished there was someone else here, because he didn't like being in this house alone. Besides it being dark and creepy, there were rats and spiders and things hiding in the walls and under the floors, and they might not be as scared of him as he was of them.

Nonetheless, he continued up to the second floor, where he peered into each room. "C.J.? Come on, I know you're here, I saw your bike outside!" But C.J. wasn't here, at least in any of the places he looked. Just all the junk he had seen before the other times he had been here, minus a couple of old *Playboy* magazines their friend Barry had taken. Tony couldn't imagine touching anything that was lying around this filthy place, much less bringing it home with him.

He reached the door to the back room, and figured C.J. must be in there. He knew C.J. sometimes liked to open one of the windows and toss food to the seagulls, watching them catch it in midair. And if that was what he was doing now, Tony thought he could give him a little scare.

He quietly turned the knob, and pushed the door till it was just slightly ajar. Then he suddenly threw it open, jumped into the room and yelled, "Gotcha!"

What he saw before him made the word die in his throat. Candy sat in an old wicker-backed chair, her hands roughly bound to the armrests, her eyes glassy with death. Blood from a large, ugly gash in her throat streamed down her body and over her torn clothes.

And as Tony took a couple of horrified steps closer, he could see a rat on her lap and another one on her arm, their snouts stained with Candy's blood.

He was now frozen, unable to comprehend what he was seeing. How could Candy be here, dead and covered with her own gore, when he had just seen her half an hour ago? Maybe even less? Just that short time ago she had been alive and happy and running, outside . . . outside, where it was safe . . .

"C.J.?" he gasped. "Anybody?" He found he could only take small steps backward, when what his mind

# NIGHTMARE

was screaming was that he should run like hell for the front door. "Oh God . . . "

He sensed the presence behind him without actually seeing anything. And he somehow knew that the person walking up behind him was not C.J., was not anyone who could help him, was in fact the person who had killed Candy.

He felt a hand, a large, strong hand, come down on his shoulder, and then another one on his throat, and that's when he was finally able to scream. But not for very long.

\*\*\*

C.J. walked off the pier and around to the front of the house, wondering where Tony was. Tony should have had plenty of time to bike over to his place and get back here in time to join C.J. in feeding the seagulls. C.J. guessed that when Tony had gotten home, his mom had given him chores to do or something, and he'd get a call from Tony later, apologizing. It was okay; they'd hang out another time.

So the sight of Tony's bicycle leaning beside his against the house confused him. So Tony had showed up. But where was he?

C.J. stepped back off the porch and yelled up at the house. "Tony! I know you're in there, I see your bike. Come on down!"

But Tony didn't. And C.J. didn't have the time to go looking for him. "I have to leave, Tony! I'm gonna go!"

This was strange. He knew Tony didn't really like this house, and found it scary, so why was in there all by himself?

"Come on, Tony, I've really gotta get going!"

There was only the sound of the wind and the seagulls, and then a passing car.

## MICHAEL GINGOLD

"Tony, if you don't come out know, I'm leaving you in there all by yourself!"

Well, if that didn't do it, nothing would. If Tony was in the house, he must not be answering on purpose, thinking it was funny. Well, the joke was on him, because he was going to leave him there alone now.

"Bye! See you tomorrow!" C.J. got on his bike and pedaled away, back toward home. He had only gone about a minute when he realized he could have hidden Tony's bike somewhere, as an extra joke. He even considered going back and doing just that, then decided against it and continued down the road.

Had he returned to the house, he would have seen the man who was standing in the upstairs window, watching him go.

\*\*\*

The kids were fighting again—about hamburgers, for God's sake.

She was making Tammy, Kim and C.J. their favorite dinner, and all they could do was squabble and yell about who was getting the biggest one.

"Gimme that one!"

"Hey, that's mine! Keep your hands off!"

"That's my hamburger!"

"No it's not!"

And then her boss had to add to the turmoil by calling just as she began serving them. "Will you be quiet?" Susan shouted at them. "I can't hear the phone!"

But they just seemed to be in a mood to bicker and yell.

"Hey, you kicked me!"

"No I didn't!"

"Mom, C.J. kicked me!"

## NIGHTMARE

"Just be quiet and eat your dinner!" she yelled, throwing a bag of buns onto the table. Then into the phone: "I'm sorry, I've got to get the kids fed. I'll call you back soon, promise."

She left the room to hang up the phone, and thus the kids saw the police cruiser pull up outside the window, lights flashing, before she did. Susan wondered why they went quiet all of a sudden, but then they started chanting, "Cop! Cop! Cop!"

She came back in and saw it too, and immediately headed for the door. The kids went silent once more as they peered out the window, and Susan went over to the cop car. She spoke briefly with the officer on the passenger side, then turned and looked at C.J.

"You're gonna get it now," Tammy said softly.

\*\*\*

Susan drove slowly down the river road, C.J. in the passenger seat, following the cruiser to the abandoned house and pulling up beside it. Another cop opened her door, and she stepped out into a flurry of activity: police and medical personnel everywhere, flashing lights, and reporters, including a TV cameraman who ran right up, attempting to capture Susan as she helped C.J. out of the driver's door. The cop beside her, whose mustache made him look like Burt Reynolds, pushed the video jockey away, and a woman with a still camera tried to take his place as Susan looked around, unsure of where to go.

Then she saw Chief Cotter beckoning to her from beside one of the ambulances. He was in his street clothes, as if he'd been abruptly pulled from his home just as she had. The look on his face was grim, and Susan knew that whatever had happened was worse than the cops had let on at their house. They had only said there was a serious situation, and that C.J.'s presence had been requested by their superiors. She suspected he had pulled another prank that had gone wrong, but C.J. would say nothing on the drive over.

As she got closer, she saw the gurney with a sheet-covered body atop it next to the ambulance, and realized things were very bad indeed.

"I'm very sorry to call you out here," Cotter said.

"Does C.J. have to be here?"

"I'm afraid he does. C.J.?"

Cotter pulled back the sheet just enough to uncover Tony's head. The boy had only a couple of small abrasions on his face, but it was clear that he was dead. C.J. gasped, and Susan cried out, taking her son in her arms.

"You know him, don't you?" When C.J. didn't respond, Cotter repeated the question, but all C.J. could do was step out of his mother's embrace, and stare at the body of his best friend.

Cotter looked down and decided it was best to cover the Walker boy back up. It was obvious C.J. did know him, and hopefully he knew more than that.

"How old are you, C.J.?"

C.J. said nothing at first.

"Is your age a secret?"

"Nine." It was barely audible over all the activity around them.

"Nine. You're a pretty big boy for nine. I'll bet you're smart, too. C.J., I need your help. I need to know what happened to your friend Tony today. Do you know anything about what happened?"

C.J. said nothing, and Susan put a hand on his shoulder and said softly, "C.J.?"

"You must have seen something," Cotter continued. "You were here with Tony, weren't you? His

# NIGHTMARE

mom said he was coming to see you at this house today. Did you see him here today?"

But C.J. couldn't answer. He hadn't actually seen Tony before, just his bike. But how could he tell them that he had just taken off, and left Tony alone with whoever or whatever it was that killed him? They'd say it was his fault, and C.J. thought they were probably right.

"C.J., please answer me. I have to know, and I have to know now. Did you see what happened to your friend Tony?"

Finally, he was able to say a simple "No."

"Are you sure? Did you see anyone else in the house?"

He hadn't, but as he thought about it, he knew for sure who had done it. It was that man, the one who'd been following him, the one who killed that lady he was dragging across the beach. He thought at first he should tell them, but then he realized that Mom would say it was just one of his stories, and the cops wouldn't believe him any more than she or Bob did.

So he just shook his head slowly.

"When was the last time you saw Tony?"

That he could tell them. "Today. Out on the road, on his bike."

"You didn't play with him at this house? His mother said you were going to be here together."

"No."

"You didn't play a trick on him? You didn't hurt Tony, did you?"

"What are you saying?" Susan exclaimed, and C.J. said defiantly, "I would never hurt Tony! He was my best friend! You can ask anybody!"

Susan drew him closer and put a comforting hand on his shoulder. "I didn't hurt him," C.J. said again, softly.

"Of course you didn't," Susan said, and then to Cotter, her voice shaking, "What are you trying to imply?"

"Susan, I know he likes to play pranks. My officers have been at your house more than once about it."

"He would never do that to Tony. Didn't you hear him say Tony was his best friend?"

Cotter paused, then motioned to one side. "Can I talk to you a moment?"

"Just for a moment." She looked down at C.J. "Stay right here, okay? I'll be right back."

"Keep the cameras away from him," Cotter told one of the cops, then led Susan over to the end of the porch, away from the lights.

"Susan, Tony wasn't the only one. There was a young woman's body upstairs too."

"Oh, God. Who was she?"

"I can't say, we're just now notifying her next of kin. But I've got two people killed here, and so far the only person I've got even an inkling might know something is your son."

"I can appreciate what you're trying to do, but this is a lot for C.J. to handle. Can't you talk to him another time?"

"I'd like to find out as much as he knows while it's still fresh in his mind."

"He just told you he doesn't know anything. He didn't see anything happen to Tony."

"And C.J. always tells the truth?"

Under other circumstances, Susan might have berated Cotter for that. Instead, she said, "You know what he does? He makes things up, he exaggerates. He tells stories about things that didn't happen. If he saw something today, he would say so, especially since it happened to Tony."

# NIGHTMARE

"Or maybe it scared him quiet."

"Well, either way, you . . . interrogating him here isn't going to get him to talk. I'm taking him home, and I'll see if he remembers anything tomorrow. If he does, I'll let you know."

She walked away without giving Cotter a chance to reply, and returned to C.J., who looked pale and scared. "Come on, C.J." she said, and led him back to the car, the cop with the Burt Reynolds mustache following. Behind her, she heard Cotter say, "Let's get him in. Okay, let's wrap it up, let's go!"

Susan got C.J. into the passenger seat, put on his seatbelt and then her own. He still looked stunned, and as started the engine he said quietly, "I'm sorry."

"It's okay. Let's just get home."

# THE FINAL DAY

**GEORGE'S SLEEP WAS** restless even without the dreams. He'd been careless, and he knew it. He should have hidden the bodies of the girl and the young boy, but he hadn't expected them to be discovered so quickly. He hadn't, in fact, expected anyone to be in the old house at all. When he happened upon it, it seemed like the perfect place to hole up, close enough to the other house that he could walk there and back, and no one to disturb him.

He hadn't expected not just one but two people to come snooping around that very day. When he heard the girl come in, he had crept to the upstairs room; his immediate urge was to attack her before he realized that keeping his presence here secret was more important. Then she walked right into that room, and she had seen him and he had seen her and—

*—she was slapping his father, beating him, why was she treating him that way, why did it seem like she was trying to kill him?*

And he had reacted immediately, the knife in his hand and tearing through her throat before he could even think about it. He had just secured her body in the chair when he heard another intruder downstairs, and there was nothing he could do but hope this boy didn't also enter the room, but . . .

# NIGHTMARE

Afterwards, he knew he shouldn't try to dispose of the corpses now, to remove them from the house in the middle of a sunny day right beside a well-traveled road. He'd come back later, and take them out under the cover of night.

But he should have hidden them away better, because when he returned, he saw the police lights from a distance, and didn't need to get closer to know that his victims had been found. So it was back to the motel, where he could be sure he'd be alone, no one and nothing to trouble him there.

Until he got into bed and closed his eyes, and his thoughts became racked with doubt. Now that they'd found those bodies, would they find him too? *Of course not*, another part of his brain shot back. Nobody even knew he was here, so how could they connect the murders to him? It wasn't like in Brooklyn, where he'd made the mistake of killing people in the same house where he lived. They wouldn't get him that easily this time.

He eventually calmed himself to the point where he could sleep—and then the nightmare had come again. He awoke stifling a scream, and grabbed the pill bottle lying beside the bed. It was a reflex, as the pills no longer worked, but he gulped down a double dose anyway. It hadn't done much good, and he wound up a sweaty, distraught mess on floor, foamy spittle forming at the corners of his mouth as he tried not to make so much noise that he woke up one of his neighbors.

After a while, the horrible images faded from his mind's eye, but at this point, sleeping was an impossibility. George hurriedly pulled some clothes on and left the room, hoping a walk in the cool night air would further soothe him. And it did, somewhat. He didn't see a single soul as he made his way down the road, ending up in a little park with a couple of benches. Taking a seat, he looked toward the horizon, which was just starting to lighten, and decided he would head back just as dawn broke, before the sun was up and the street came back to life.

A couple of cars passed as he sat there, taking deep breaths of the night air. One of them he heard before he saw, as loud music was thumping from inside. It slowed as it neared the park, then stopped, though there was no traffic sign or light.

George didn't move or react as the car sat idling, and couldn't see anything through the windows. Were the occupants looking for trouble? Did they think he was some drunk fresh from an open-all-night bar, and an easy mark? If so, George smirked at the thought of the big surprise they had coming to them.

Instead, the car accelerated and sped off. He watched it go, then glanced back toward the horizon, where orange was now bleeding up into the pale blue of the distant sky. It was time to go back, and try to get a little more sleep.

He was passing a side street a few blocks from the motel when he saw something that brought him to a dead stop, then quickly stepped up against the building beside him. Carefully looking around the corner, he confirmed what he had spotted in the dawning light.

His car was parked halfway down that side street, and behind it was a police car. Two officers had gotten out and were inspecting the vehicle, one shining a flashlight through the windshield.

George fought the panic building inside him. They'd found it. He'd been careful to park in a spot with no restrictions or time limits, just as he'd been careful not to park too close to the motel. So if the cops were examining it, they must know it was stolen.

# NIGHTMARE

But still, how could they possibly tie it to him? He'd made sure not to leave anything inside of his own, just paperwork in the glove compartment belonging to its now-deceased owner. But fingerprints—they could pull his fingerprints. In all his careful planning, he hadn't had the presence of mind to wipe down the steering wheel and door handles. How had that not occurred to him before, when it had come to mind so quickly now?

No matter. He knew he had to leave this area, at least for a while. He'd find another car, and do it tonight.

But first, there was one other place he had to go. He wasn't going to depart until he'd finished what he came here to do.

\*\*\*

The muttering and the looks started the moment C.J. walked in the front door and down the elementary-school hall with Tammy and Kim, holding his books close to him. His hopes that somehow, the news about last night's events hadn't gotten around town, or at least to the other kids, were quickly dashed, and he tried to ignore the stares as he made his way to his homeroom. He wished Tammy and Kim could stay with him, but they had different homerooms upstairs, and as they separated, Tammy gave him a genuinely sympathetic look and said, "We'll see you at lunch, okay?"

C.J. said nothing, just proceeded to his homeroom, where he took his usual seat. It was in the second row, and he truly wanted to sit in the back today, but changing his place would just attract more attention to him, and he didn't want any more of that right now.

The rest of his classmates filed in, and as the room

filled, C.J. couldn't help but keep glancing at the empty seat beside his. He wondered if Mrs. Baker would say anything about it before she took attendance.

She didn't, but she didn't have to. C.J. could hear the whispering around and behind him, and even at that low volume, he could tell quite a bit of it was coming from that jerk Peter Bergstrom. Peter was always giving him a hard time, and C.J. knew he was going to be a lot worse today.

When Mrs. Baker called his name, C.J. said "Here" as normally as he could, then waited to see if she would accidentally call Tony's name. She didn't, and instead turned to the chalkboard to start outlining the day's lesson. She hadn't taken her eyes off the class for more than a few seconds before something lightly struck C.J.'s arm and dropped to the floor beside him.

It was a wadded-up piece of notebook paper, and it seemed to have come from Peter's direction. Without looking around, C.J. picked it up, opened and flattened it out on his desk.

On the paper was a crude drawing of a standing figure with "C.J." written next to it, and a figure lying dead with "Tony" written beside it. Streams of red were drawn coming off of "Tony" in colored pencil.

C.J. knew his mom would say he should ignore it, like kids should ignore all bullies. But he also knew that old advice didn't work in the real world. He crumped the paper back up, turned and hurled it at Peter. Unfortunately, Mrs. Baker turned around just then and caught him.

"C.J.! What are you doing?"

"He threw it at me first!"

"No I didn't!" Peter insisted.

"Yes you did, I saw you." That wasn't true, but Mrs. Baker couldn't know that.

# NIGHTMARE

"Yeah?" Peter sneered. "Well, at least I wasn't trying to kill you!"

That brought stifled laughter from a few of the other kids, and gasps from a couple of others. And it made Mrs. Baker angry, which C.J. appreciated.

"Peter, that's not fair and it's not appropriate," she said sternly. "I want you to apologize to C.J."

"But Mrs. Baker, he threw it at me!"

"Apologize, Peter."

"Fine. I'm sorry Tony's dead, and C.J. killed him."

"Peter! You go to the office, right now!"

"Great," Peter said as he got up from his desk. "He's a criminal but I'm getting punished."

"Go!"

Peter did. C.J. hoped the trouble was over, but then Laura Farnsworth had to open her mouth.

"Mrs. Baker, how come he's here after what he did?" she asked with the absolute assurance of a 10-year-old expert, likely one who'd been discussing the subject with her parents.

"Laura, we don't know that he did anything."

"Maybe *you* don't know," Laura shot back.

"All right, that's enough," Mrs. Baker said. "C.J., would you please come with me?"

There was kindness in her tone, and C.J. felt there was no reason to argue. He picked up his books and joined her in exiting the classroom. She departed with, "I want everyone to behave till I get back!"

"So we can misbehave when you do?" Randy Meisner cracked, drawing a round of chuckles. Mrs. Baker ignored him as she took C.J. down to the guidance office to find him a ride home.

\*\*\*

Dr. Williamson hurried through the main terminal of Orlando International Airport, weaving his way through the throngs of arriving and departing tourists. If only he could be among them, instead of having to travel down here for reasons he didn't even believe were necessary. Hell, he had felt like the only adult on the plane who wasn't taking one or more kids on vacation to Disney World. And having to rebook his flight at the last minute hadn't helped.

As he made his way through the main waiting area, he strained to recognize a familiar face. Then a man he didn't recognize, wearing a cream-colored suit, waved and strode over to greet him.

"Dr. Williamson?"

"Yes."

"Burt Daniels." They shook hands. "How was your flight?"

"Good. I'm just glad I was able to switch it."

They began walking toward the exit, Daniels' stride fast and purposeful, which squared with how Jackson had described him.

"So you don't think he's in Daytona Beach now?" Dr. Williamson continued.

"The Stockton car was found in Cocoa Beach first thing this morning. There was an APB put out on it for this entire region."

"Any sign of Tatum?"

"Not yet. The initial search of the car gave us nothing, but forensics is going over it now."

"Is there any conclusive proof he even stole that car?"

"Not yet. But I've been doing some digging, and I've come up with some very interesting information."

"This still doesn't make sense to me. I just don't believe he would travel this far."

"You will, Dr. Williamson."

They reached the exit, and Daniels led Dr.

# NIGHTMARE

Williamson out to a car parked right outside the doors. As he went to get in, Dr. Williamson saw Jackson sitting in the back seat, complete with cigar. Shit. He'd hoped that Jackson had gone on to Cocoa Beach already, and he and Daniels would meet him there. Now he'd have to share the trip with Jackson and his damn stogie.

As they left the airport and got onto 528 East for the hour's drive, he knew that convincing one of them, much less both, that they were looking in the wrong place would be a fruitless effort. But he had to try.

"George is not here," he said as civilization gave way to woods on either side of the highway. "I have known George for quite some time. He's my patient, I know his patterns, I know the way he thinks . . ."

"Paul, Paul," Daniels tried to interrupt, but Dr. Williamson wasn't finished.

"He tries to stay in familiar surroundings . . ."

"I checked the family name, Paul!"

"He can't be down here!"

"I checked the family name!" Daniels repeated. "It's a very unusual name in this neck of the woods."

"But we know that a family with the same name has lived in this area," Jackson chimed in.

"So?" Dr. Williamson asked, incredulous that this was their evidence. "It's a coincidence, nothing more."

"Not at all," Jackson said. "In fact, they've lived in several different areas down here."

"Which is exactly why I had such trouble tracking them," Daniels picked up, almost as if he and Jackson had practiced it. "But there is a connection."

"There is no connection!"

"Paul, there is a solid connection," Daniels said. "This man is in Florida."

"On the basis of him having the same name?"

Were these two hiding something? Dr. Williamson was about to start pressing them before Jackson said, "Let me make it real simple for you, Paul. George's recurring dream? Something very similar happened around here 25 years ago. It's all in the police records Daniels dug up."

"Twenty-five years ago?" Dr. Williamson said. "He would have been a . . . "

He trailed off as he realized he was about to prove their point.

"That's right," Jackson said. "It really happened, here! His father, his mother, both murdered. They even determined it was done with an ax! It's the same person, Paul. It is George Tatum."

"Assuming you're right, then what the hell happened to him after that?"

"He was put into the foster care system," Daniels said. "From there, his trail goes cold. So far."

Jackson leaned in closer to them. "It doesn't matter. He has roots in this area, he's had recurring dreams about exactly that kind of double murder. His car was found in Myrtle Beach, and the car of a woman who went missing in Myrtle Beach just turned up here. Do we have to connect any more dots for you, Paul?"

Dr. Williamson had nothing to say to that, but Daniels had to rub it in by adding, "Psychiatric speculation is no match for good old-fashioned investigative work."

Dr. Williamson thought that Daniels' investigations were anything but old-fashioned, but he was right. It appeared they were both right. His patient was here, and God knows what he'd been up to.

"All right," he said. "So what do we do now?"

"What we have to try and do here is map out—" Daniels began, but Jackson cut him off.

# NIGHTMARE

"We don't have to map out anything. Paul, you believed in these drugs. You told us you were rebuilding this man. But now he's back out in the world, and he's clearly killed again. At least once. And we can't have that, Paul. We can't have him killing, we can't have him traced back to the program. Now, you find him, and you fix it."

Find him and fix it. Jackson made it sound easy, and Dr. Williamson knew it would be anything but.

\*\*\*

Susan tried not to raise her voice. She had taken a break and was in the back room of the store, where fortunately there was a phone extension, but she was still concerned about anyone up front hearing her.

"Kathy, I am desperate," she said. "I've called everybody I know, everybody there is. Please, just come tonight."

"I told you, Mrs. Temper," Kathy replied. "I can't take him anymore. I just can't be around him. Especially with what people are saying about him now."

"That's all bullshit. He would never have hurt his friend. And he's . . . changed since last night. He's not going to give you any trouble."

"What's so important that you can't stay home with him?"

"There's a business party for Bob, and—"

"A party? That's all it is?"

"Someone's going to be there who Bob wants to introduce me to. It's important, Kathy, I promise you. I wouldn't be asking otherwise."

"I'm sorry, Mrs. Temper, it's not worth it."

"I'll make it worth your while, Kathy. I'll pay you double. I know you need the money."

Kathy was quiet, which made Susan hopeful. "It'll

just be two hours. And I promise you again, C.J. won't cause any more trouble. Please, Kathy, just this one more time?"

There was a pause before Kathy said flatly, "Okay. Just this once."

"Thank you, Kathy, you don't know how much I appreciate this."

"I'll see you later," Kathy said, and hung up.

Susan truly was grateful. At first, she had told Bob to go to the party without her, but when he mentioned that one of the best psychiatrists in the area would be one of the guests, who could either help C.J. or might know someone who could, she was convinced to go.

And as she had told Kathy, C.J. did seem different now. Not better, certainly; seeing Tony lying on that gurney had absolutely been a shock to him, and when they had gotten back to the house, he had run right upstairs and gone to bed. This morning he had been quiet, obedient, insisting he was okay. She had let him go off to school reluctantly, with Tammy and Kim promising they'd look out for him.

But he still clearly needed more help than she could give him, and she hoped she would find it at the party tonight. She hung up the phone and went back out into the store.

\*\*\*

C.J. walked up to the front door and checked under the welcome mat. Thank goodness, the key was there this time. He held it up so Mrs. Lambert could see it, and she waved and backed her car out of the driveway. C.J. was thankful she had given him a ride to the house, even though he had to sit in the guidance office for over an hour until she could take an early lunch break to do it.

Upstairs, in Susan's room, George didn't hear the

# NIGHTMARE

door open and close below. He was fixated on what was in his hands right now: a pair of pink panties he had withdrawn from the chest of drawers. He fondled them, rubbing them between his hands, aroused by their silky softness, imagining her wearing them, wearing *only* them, until he took them in his hands and slid them down her beautiful legs, off of her feet, and now she was naked and he could—

"Mom, are you home?" The boy's voice from downstairs startled him, and he dropped the panties to the floor. What was he doing here now? He should be at . . .

"The school sent me home. They all think I killed Tony!" So that was it. The boy was back, and wasn't leaving. He needed to hide for now and figure out what to do next.

He replaced the panties in the drawer and slowly closed it. It went silently—until it fell into place with a wooden *clunk*.

"Are you up there?" came the voice from below. The boy had heard that, and now he had to act fast. George slipped out of the bedroom and over to the closet, where he pulled the door as closed as he could without the latchbolt clicking home and making another sound.

Stepping back, shrouding himself in the hanging clothes, he heard nothing more at first. Then footsteps, as the boy came up the stairs and—

*—he was coming up the stairs, his brain buzzing with anger, not comprehending what he had seen but knowing how he could put a stop to it . . .*

George stifled a cry of anguish and dug into his pocket, coming up with the pill bottle. They weren't likely to work, but it was the only thing he could do.

"Are you up here?" The boy was literally right

outside the closet, but fortunately walked right past it. George heard him knock on a door. "You're in here, aren't you?" The sound of the door opening, a beat of silence, and then the boy continuing down the hall. "Mom?"

Shaking now, George opened the bottle. Only five pills left, and he felt he would have to take them all if they were going to have any effect. He spilled them into his hand, but it was so unsteady that they flew right out and into the hallway, dropping onto the carpet right outside the closet.

He could reach down and grab them, quickly, while the boy was checking the rooms. But what if the boy just happened to turn in this direction? What if he was spotted?

And in the time it took those thoughts to pass through his mind, he heard the boy coming back this way. He retreated as far back into the closet as he could, until his back touched wood.

The boy walked into view and stopped, looking at the floor curiously. He kneeled down, picked up the pills and went down the stairs.

In the closet, George struggled with his breathing and his thoughts. That had been close, and he couldn't risk the boy discovering him again. He had to get him out of here somehow . . .

Downstairs, C.J. sat at a table, arranging the pills into little patterns. He didn't know what he was going to do until Mom got home; there was nothing to watch on TV this time of day, and he didn't feel like reading. He couldn't call any of his friends, because they were all in school, and anyway they probably all thought he'd killed Tony too. Why did everyone think that? How could they think he'd do that to his best friend in the world? Sure, he'd pulled scary pranks on them a

# NIGHTMARE

couple of times, but they were just jokes. They were funny. How come no one could tell the difference?

The phone rang, and he slid the pills into one hand, dropped them in a pocket, and answered it. "Hello?"

"Leave this house," said the voice on the other end. It sounded like the person on the other end was scared, as well as trying to scare him. "Now . . . while you can . . . "

"Peter, is that you?" C.J. said. That's who it had to be, pranking C.J. for getting him sent home from school. "What do you think you're doing? You don't scare me at all!"

"Get out of here! Get out!" the voice insisted. But C.J. wasn't about to go anywhere, especially when he knew who it was. He hung up the phone, then stuck his tongue out at it. Stupid Peter. If he called back, he'd tell Peter he was going to kill him next, and see how fast Peter hung up then.

He was all prepared to do that when the phone rang again a few minutes later. But when he answered, the voice on the other end was his mother's. "C.J.? Are you all right? The school called and told me what happened."

"I'm all right. Are you gonna be home soon?"

"I'm sorry, I can't. I have to stay at work. And then I have to go somewhere afterwards."

"You won't be home for dinner?"

"No, I'm so sorry. But Kathy will come over, and—"

"She's coming back? You're going out with Bob again, aren't you?"

"C.J., this is really important, okay? I have to meet with someone tonight, and Kathy will take care of you and your sisters."

"I don't want her here. I want you."

"I'll explain this all to you later, I promise. Just . . . be good for Kathy tonight, all right? I'll see you later."

"Fine."

It sounded like she might say more, but C.J. hung up at that point. So Mom was going out again, even after what happened. He found he couldn't even get angry. He just felt . . . empty. Like he didn't want to do anything now.

He wandered into the TV room, plopped down in front of the set, turned it on and started flipping the knob, trying to find something to watch.

Upstairs, George had heard enough of the conversation to know that she wasn't going to be home for a while. That it would be just the boy, then his sisters and then the babysitter. He knew he would have to stay up here, hidden, till sometime possibly late into the night.

And he didn't know if he could hold out that long.

\*\*\*

The party was, as Susan expected, an awkward time for her. Word had clearly gotten around fast about C.J.'s presence at the site of the murders yesterday, and though no one came out and said anything, she saw the looks and could almost hear the whispers. She knew from the moment she arrived that she wanted to keep a low profile, to let Bob do his hobnobbing and networking, and only introduce herself with her first name. There was only one person here besides Bob whom she really wanted to talk to, and she was relieved when, over an hour after they arrived, Bob was finally able to make the introduction.

"It's nice to meet you, Dr. Andrews," she said to the bespectacled man in the good suit and bad tie, as they and Bob stood by the far end of the swimming pool behind the house.

# NIGHTMARE

"It's nice to meet you too. I'm very sorry to hear about your troubles."

"How much has Bob told you?"

"Enough to know that your concerns would have been very different if we had met two nights ago. How is your son coping?"

"I wish I could tell you for sure. He's been quieter, better-behaved, but that was just this morning. He says he's okay, but . . ."

"But you don't believe that."

"He lost his best friend in the worst possible way. I don't feel equipped to help him with that."

"And Bob tells me that just the other day, he pretended to have been stabbed himself?"

"Among other things. He just has this fixation lately on scaring people, and telling these crazy stories. It was driving me crazy too. And now this."

"You say lately. How long has this been going on?"

"I guess since last summer."

Dr. Andrews glanced at Bob when she said that, then back at her. "Ordinarily, I'd say a boy his age being interested in scary things is nothing to worry about. Boys that age like to test themselves, to see how much they can take. And sometimes how much their parents can take, too."

"Well, he's certainly pushed that limit."

"And now he's been confronted with the most frightening reality possible."

"Do you think that—I mean, I hate to put it this way, but do you think it might have scared him straight?"

"I couldn't say for sure until I spoke to him myself."

"So you'll see him?"

"Absolutely." He took a small metal case out of a

pocket and handed her a business card. "Call my office on Monday. We'll set up an appointment with you and your son."

"Thank you, doctor. I really appreciate the help."

"It's what I'm here for," he said with a smile.

"And . . . I hate to ask this, but can you tell me what your rate would be?"

"We'll discuss that on Monday also. It was nice to meet you." He extended a hand and she shook it, and then he was off into the thick of the party.

"Thanks," she said to Bob.

"My pleasure. I think he can do C.J. a lot of good."

"I hope so. I just hope he's behaving for Kathy tonight."

"He's probably already asleep." Bob put an arm around Susan's shoulders. "Let's go get you another drink."

\*\*\*

Kathy carefully opened the bedroom door, and was relieved to see C.J. conked out in his bed. He could always be faking it, but he had seemed a lot more subdued than usual tonight, doing what he was told and getting along with his sisters, who seemed genuinely concerned for him.

When she'd heard about Tony's death, she couldn't help thinking that C.J. was in fact somehow responsible—not that he had intentionally killed his friend, but that one of his pranks had gone badly wrong. She was in a better position than anyone to understand just how far he could take his scare tactics.

Then, a little while after she spoke to Mrs. Temper, one of her friends called with the news that Candy Benedict had also been found dead in that house, and her feelings changed. There was no way C.J. could be responsible for that. In fact, she now felt

# NIGHTMARE

it odd that Mrs. Temper would go out somewhere that very night and not stay home with her kids, and have her boyfriend come over for extra protection. To be honest, Kathy wasn't entirely comfortable being in this house tonight, not far from the murder scene, though she was reassured by the fact that on the way over, there were still a few cops at the old house, continuing their investigation. If he was smart, the killer would have fled far away from here by now.

Still, she double-checked the locks on all the doors and windows on the ground floor before going upstairs to look in on all the kids. Like C.J., Tammy and Kim were fast asleep, and she headed back down to the TV room to see if there was anything interesting on.

She got nothing but some dumb sitcom, a show about local rich people and their yachts, and commercials. She settled on the latter and sat down in one of the chairs, waiting to see what would come on. When it did, a terrified woman was screaming and fleeing from a man in dark clothes and a ski mask. This was not what she wanted to see right now, and she stood up to change the channel.

Before she could move further, she was seized from behind. She let out a little shriek of terror as strong hands spun her around, and it was cut off as she was kissed hard on the mouth.

Kathy relaxed as she realized who it was. She returned the kiss for a few moments, then broke free.

"My God, Joey. What are you trying to do, pull a C.J. on me?"

Joey gave her that smile that always made her unable to stay mad at him for long. "Hey, don't get so upset, babe. My sister told me where you were."

"How'd you get in here? All the doors were locked."

"That side door wasn't that hard to get through."

"Oh my God." She hurried over to that door, which Joey had left standing ajar, and closed it, securing the lock. "You realize there's a murderer running around?"

"That doesn't scare me. Besides, I'm here to protect you now."

"My strong man."

"You know it, babe."

She returned to him, and they embraced and kissed some more, and she actually did feel safer now, with his well-muscled arms around her.

"We can get high later on," he whispered. "I brought a joint over."

"I don't know. The kids are upstairs."

"Aren't they asleep?"

"Yeah, I just checked on 'em. But what if they wake up?"

"Don't worry. I can be quiet if you can."

He kissed her again, those strong hands pulling up her T-shirt and caressing her back. "I'll cover your mouth if I have to."

"Joey, God! I don't believe you."

"I've missed you, Kathy. You cancelled out on me the other night, you cancelled out on me tonight."

"I told you, I was making some extra money. Especially tonight."

"Well, I just couldn't wait."

He picked her up and carried her into the living room. There was no light in here save for some dwindling flames in the fireplace, and he almost tripped on something on the floor.

"Watch it!" Kathy laughed. "What are you trying to do, kill us both?"

They tumbled to the floor, Kathy landing on top

of Joey. Their arms went around each other, and she kissed him hard, her tongue wrestling with his. It had indeed been a little while since they'd really gotten to explore each other's company, and as long as they didn't wake the kids . . .

She pulled off his shirt and he pulled off hers, roughly, sending buttons flying. Her bra came next, and they embraced and there was the delicious feeling of skin on skin as he kissed her deeper, and she kissed him back. Then his lips were on her neck, and he was kissing his way down to her breasts, his tongue flicking across her nipples as she bit her tongue to keep from crying out.

When she couldn't take the teasing anymore she grabbed his shoulders, flipping him onto his back, and undid his belt and the snap on his jeans. Joey raised his legs so she could pull his pants off easily, tossing them aside, followed by his briefs. He sat up suddenly, lunging at her, slipping his fingers into her panties and yanking them down. Then he yanked her down, and she went willingly and he was on top of her again, inside her.

She wrapped her legs around him as he thrust into her, slowly at first, then faster and harder, building up the intensity just the way she liked it until his body was slapping against hers. His breath was hot and loud in her ear as she moaned and gasped, not thinking about the kids anymore, not thinking about anything but how good it felt to have Joey ravishing her.

Her eyes closed tight, she didn't see the tall figure slowly emerging from the stairwell, gazing at them as they thrashed the lust out of each other, until their sounds of passion slowed and quieted. By the time she opened her eyes, the figure was gone.

Joey rolled off of Kathy and they lay by the dying

fire, holding hands, enjoying their lingering arousal. Finally Joey murmured, "I could go with another joint right now."

"Is that what you want more of?" Kathy said with a little laugh.

"Hey, give me a little time to get my strength back."

He sat up and looked around the darkened room. "Where did you throw my pants?"

"What do you want your pants for?"

"That's where the joint is."

She chuckled again, pointing to a corner of the room. "They're over there."

"How 'bout going and getting that joint for me?"

"Get it yourself." She sat up too. "I'm going to take a shower."

"I've got to do everything by myself, huh?"

"I'm sure you'll manage."

She stood and went to the stairs, and Joey watched as her gorgeous body caught the light from the kitchen before she headed up. Smiling, he turned back to the task at hand.

"Here, pants. Where are you?" He crawled across the floor, thought he had found them but then realized otherwise. "Nope, you're a shirt. I'm looking for my pants, have you seen 'em?" He kept feeling around ahead of him until his hand fell upon the denim.

"What do you know, my pants! Now, where's that smoke?" It didn't take him long to extricate the joint and a lighter from one of the pockets, and he quickly had it blazing and took a nice, deep inhale.

"That's the good stuff," he sighed. He let out the smoke in a long breath, then took another toke.

It was the last breath he would ever take, because in the next instant, something snapped around his neck and tightened. His cry of fear was cut off as he

# NIGHTMARE

was pulled up and dragged back, trying vainly to get to his feet, clutching at his throat. He felt thick metal wire and sharp metal barbs, and it got even tighter as the smoke he'd inhaled burned in his lungs. He couldn't breathe it out, he couldn't breathe at all and now his lungs were on fire and his vision was starting to cloud.

With his last burst of strength, Joey planted his feet and pushed up, and whoever had ahold of the wire pulled back on it violently and he fell. The wire around his neck caught him, and he could feel blood trickling from where the barbs had punctured his skin, and it seemed like his head would tear loose from his body.

Instead, his vision went dark and his head lolled back and he went motionless. The figure gripping the wire held on a little longer, just to be sure, before letting Joey fall dead to the floor.

\*\*\*

Kathy got out of the shower, wrapped herself in a towel, and opened the bathroom door partway. The usual routine, except this time, she wouldn't be interrupted by one of C.J.'s tricks. She had checked on him again just before going for her shower, and he was still asleep, just as he had been before. He looked peaceful, and she felt a twinge of sympathy for him, even after everything he'd put her through. The poor kid had been through a lot in the last day.

She dried herself off, wrapped a towel around her hair and replaced the one around her body with a robe. The shower had refreshed her, and she was ready for another round with Joey, if he was up for it. She'd heard that marijuana was good for the libido, so the joint he was puffing in the living room might help.

When she entered that room, though, he was nowhere to be seen, smoking or not. "Joey? Where'd you go?"

Squinting, she could see that his clothes were all still strewn around, so he couldn't have gone outside. Was he hiding somewhere, waiting to give her another scare? If he was, that was going to kill the mood nice and quick.

"Joey, come on. I'm not in the mood for jokes now. Come on out."

She looked over to the couch on the far side of the room. It was the only piece of furniture in here big enough to hide him, and she made her way over to it quietly. Maybe she could give him a little jump instead.

Crouching down, she crept up till she was practically on top of the couch, then jumped up onto the cushions, looking down behind it. "Gotcha!"

Even in the gloom, she could tell he wasn't there. This was starting to piss her off, and if he thought this was going to help him get some more, he was mistaken.

She was both startled and, for a split second, relieved when she turned and saw the person standing on the other side of the room. For that briefest bit of time, her mind registered it as Joey. Then she realized it was that damned mask. The body was shrouded in shadow, but the mask was visible enough for her to recognize as the one she had last seen in the bathroom mirror.

"C.J.! What are you doing out of bed?" Fury was rising in her now. Here he was, pulling one of his stunts again, after what he'd been through. And to think she had felt sorry for him.

"I'm sick and tired of your silly games! Will you knock it off?"

There was no answer, no movement. Just that mask, seeming to float in the darkness, leering at her.

"OK, that's it. I'm calling your mother."

# NIGHTMARE

She went for the phone that she knew sat on the desk beside the couch, even though she could barely see it. As her hand reached the receiver, she saw the mask move out of the corner of her eye, and it was atop a tall body, a body that couldn't be C.J.'s, and it ran across the room at lightning speed. Her wrist was pinned to the desk so she couldn't lift the receiver, and with its other hand her attacker raised a rock hammer and brought the pick slamming down into her arm.

Kathy screamed as the metal punched through her flesh and bone, blood spurting from the wound. She tried to pull away but couldn't, and she looked with terrified eyes at the mask and it wasn't C.J., his pranks had just been warnings, trying to get her to stay away from this house, trying to keep her from being here on this particular night, but she hadn't heeded the warnings and now it was too late . . .

The pick was wrenched from her arm, and in the next instant it punched into her chest, again and again. Kathy fell back, blood streaming from the wounds and staining the robe, eyes wide and mouth gaping in disbelief. She tried to scream again but couldn't, there was no more breath left in her, and she collapsed against the wall and slowly slid down, leaving a smear of blood behind. She was dead before her head reached the floor.

Standing across the room, at the base of the stairs, C.J. stood in his pajamas, staring in horror. The masked man stood over Kathy's body, staring down at her, his breathing coarse and heavy. He was wearing a dark suit, and C.J., in his shock, didn't even relate him to the trenchcoated stranger he had been sure was following him. This was someone else, a random intruder who had destroyed his babysitter and would no doubt come after him next.

The man began turning toward him, and C.J. bolted up the stairs and down the hall to his sisters' room. Throwing open the door and flipping on the light, he screamed, "Kim! Tammy! Wake up! Someone just killed Kathy!"

Startled out of her sleep, Tammy rubbed her eyes. "Get out of here! Go back to your room!"

"I'm not lying! Kathy's dead, he killed her! He's coming up here!"

"If this is a joke, you're really gonna get it," Tammy said as Kim sat up next to her, looking scared.

"I swear to God, this isn't a joke!" C.J. cried, and just then came the sound of the phone ringing from another room. He knew he couldn't go to answer it right away, and instead pulled Tammy and Kim off their bed. "Come on! Now!"

He led them across the hall and into his room, slammed the door and locked it as the phone continued to ring.

\*\*\*

Sitting in the upstairs bedroom as the party continued below her, Susan wondered why it was taking so long for Kathy to answer the phone. The kids should be in bed by now, with nothing else to distract Kathy from picking up. She was starting to become concerned when the ring was suddenly interrupted.

"Kathy? What took you so long to answer? Are the kids asleep?"

She heard nothing on the other end, other than what sounded like muffled breathing. "Kathy? Kathy, please say something!"

No one did, Kathy or otherwise. "C.J.? C.J., if this is you, you'd better talk to me!"

Now even the breathing stopped. There was complete silence, and the line went dead. In the next

# NIGHTMARE

second, Susan had slapped the receive back into its cradle and was running downstairs to find Bob.

***

C.J. leaped across his mother's bed to grab the phone beside it. Yanking the receiver to his ear, he yelled, "Mom? Mom!"

But all he heard was a dial tone. Whoever it was, he had just missed them. Jumping off the bed, he hurried to get back to his sisters—and stopped short. A shadow fell across the floor outside the bedroom door, slowly moving down the hall.

C.J. grabbed the door, slammed it shut and locked it. He hoped the noise would lead the intruder to come after him instead of Tammy and Kim, but he knew he only had a matter of minutes before the man would find his way inside. And sure enough, as he pulled open the top drawer of the clothes chest, there was a *bang* on the door and the tip of the pick pierced through the wood. It withdrew, then burst through again, a little further this time, before it was twisted out.

Desperately rifling through each of the drawers, unable to find what he was seeking, C.J. didn't even look at the door as it was struck again and again. He could hear the wood being punctured and torn, and that was enough. Any second now, his attacker would be able to get in.

His search of the chest fruitless, he went to the bed, pulling at the covers, digging under the mattress. Behind him, the pick tore ever-bigger holes in the door, until there was one large enough for a hand, clad in a transparent rubber glove, to reach through and clutch the doorknob.

But by then, C.J. had found what he was looking for.

He raised the revolver and fired, and a spurt of blood erupted from the hand, accompanied by a cry of pain from the other side of the door. The hand withdrew, and C.J. fired again, putting a hole in the black jacket and sending the man staggering backwards. He fired a third time, and the man's body jerked and disappeared from view. A second later, C.J. heard him hit the floor.

He opened the savaged door slowly and stepped into the hallway, still holding the gun in front of him. The man lay sprawled at his feet, blood spreading outward from the bullet holes in his clothing. Training the revolver on the fallen body, C.J. waited, alert for any signs of life. None came, and he went to his room and knocked.

"Come on out, let's go!"

Tammy and Kim emerged, wrapped in blankets, and screamed when they saw the bloodied man wearing C.J.'s mask on the floor before them. "Oh my God, who is he?" Tammy squealed.

"Who cares?" C.J. shouted. "Let's get downstairs, quick!"

He darted into his room and grabbed a big red blanket off the bed, and they all hurried down and out the side door, where they stopped to catch their breath.

"Where's Kathy?" Tammy implored.

"She's dead," C.J. said flatly.

"No!" Tammy sobbed.

"Just stay here, okay? I have to call the police."

"No, don't go back in there!"

"It's okay, the phone's right there."

He went inside and picked up the phone on the wall. Keeping his eye on the stairs, he dialed 0. But instead of connecting, the steady *brrrrrrr* of the dial tone continued.

# NIGHTMARE

At first, C.J. didn't understand what was wrong. Then he realized and turned toward Tammy, who stood holding the side door open, looking pale and frightened.

"The phone's off the hook in Mom's room. I have to go hang it up."

"No, C.J., you can't! He's up there!"

"I killed him!"

"How do you know for sure?"

"Even if I didn't, I've still got the gun. I have to go in." And he went, holding the revolver in both hands. With his blue pajamas and the red blanket hanging off his shoulders, Tammy couldn't help thinking he looked like Superman.

C.J. made his way up the stairs trying to make as little noise as possible, even as he was sure there was nothing to worry about. He'd shot the man three times, and that meant he had to be dead. There was no way he could—

He came around the corner into the hallway, and the man was gone. Only some bloodstains remained.

Part of him wanted to immediately turn and run, to get back outside the house and run to the neighbors and call the police from there. Yet another part felt that he couldn't have gone very far with three shots in him, that he must have just crawled into another room.

He had weighed his options for a matter of seconds before the closet door burst open and the man flew out. C.J. screamed and tried to turn the gun on him, but the man knocked it out of his hands. He raised the rock hammer, and C.J. closed his eyes and thought *I'm so sorry Mom I'm so sorry Tammy I'm so sorry Kim* and then he was thrown into the closet, the door slammed shut before he could react. He heard the rock hammer *thunk* between the door and the frame, pinning it closed.

C.J. threw his body against the door with all his strength, but it wouldn't give. Now he was trapped and his gun was gone and the bad man was going to go after his sisters.

"Tammy! Kim!" he screamed as loud as he could. "Run! Run away, he's coming to get you!"

And he hoped against hope that they could actually hear him.

\*\*\*

George stepped back from the closet door, watching to be sure it would hold and the boy wouldn't be able to force it open. His mind barely registered the pain from the gunshots; it was focused solely on what he was going to do next. When it was clear the boy wouldn't be able to escape, he went for the stairs, meaning to get out of the house and—

*—make his way down the stairs outside, fear and confusion swirling in his mind, along with the determination of what he had to do. He went to the storage shed behind the house, where he knew the tools were kept, one in particular that he would use to punish the woman, this woman who looked like his mother but was doing such awful things to his father.*

*He entered the shed and found the axe. Picking it up, he hefted the heavy wood and metal, getting the feel of it before he started back up toward the front door.*

*He entered the house and walked up the stairs that led to the bedroom, a little part of his mind hoping he was wrong, that he'd been seeing things, that he would find his mother and father fully dressed and sitting together, holding hands or maybe kissing a little, doing things that loving parents were supposed to do.*

*Instead, he heard the slapping before he even got*

# NIGHTMARE

to the doorway. He entered the room and his father was still tied down with almost nothing on, this woman who couldn't be his mother hitting him, again and again. And his father wasn't yelling at her or telling her to stop. Why wasn't he doing that?

Well, he'd put a stop to it. He stood behind his mother and raised the axe. Putting all of his strength behind it, he swung and buried the blade in the woman's neck.

She made a horrible, choking, gurgling sound, and one of her hands flew up to the wound, is if she could stop the gush of blood issuing from it. His father screamed, "No! No! What are you doing?" but he paid that no mind.

He swung again and the axe separated his mother's head from her body. It spun in the air once and then dropped to the bed, bouncing off and coming to rest on the floor. Blood gushed upward from the neck like a geyser, spraying him and his father and the bed until it finally collapsed.

"You little bastard!" his father cried. "What did you do?" So this man couldn't be his father either. His father would never talk to him like that. He climbed up onto the bed, raised the axe and brought it down.

"Nooooo!" his father screamed as the blade sank into his chest. "Oh my God nooooo!" He brought the axe down again and again into his father's body, blood spurting forth every time he pulled it out and streaking the walls and the mirror above the bed. He raised the axe one more time and brought it down hard into his father's forehead, and the screams suddenly stopped.

George looked up into the mirror and saw his face and his clothes drenched in red, in between the splotches on the glass. He was calm now, the *confusion and anger gone. He had done right, and punished these two people he thought were his parents but had proven to be very bad people indeed.*

*He got off the bed and went over to a chair, one of the few objects in the room not touched by the blood. Sitting down, he knew he had to come up with a story, an explanation for what had happened. But he knew it wouldn't be too difficult, and it would be no problem getting people to believe that someone else had done this. After all, he was just a child . . .*

The memory that had become his recurring nightmare was abruptly penetrated by the honking of a horn. George looked out a window and saw a car pulling rapidly into the driveway, the two girls running to meet it. She was back now, and he wasn't going to wait any longer. He would get the girls out of the way somehow, and then he would finally have her. Pulling off the mask, he tossed it aside.

The car lurched to a stop and he saw Susan get out of the passenger side. And then the bearded man getting out of the driver's seat. So there was something else he'd have to take care of first. He stepped back and disappeared into the darkness of the living room.

\*\*\*

Susan and Bob could barely make out what the girls were saying, they were talking over each other so fast. But it quickly became clear that someone dangerous was in the house, someone who Tammy said had killed Kathy, and that C.J. was in there with him.

"C.J.!" Susan screamed, and made for the side door.

"Susan, wait!" Bob said, catching her arm.

"I'm not waiting. My son is in there!"

She ran inside and Bob followed, stopping her in the kitchen. "Wait a second!" He pulled open a drawer and came up with a large knife, which he handed to Susan. Then he took out one for himself.

"C.J., are you in here?" Bob yelled, and they faintly heard C.J. shouting back in response, along with sounds of pounding.

"He's upstairs," Bob said, and Susan was already hurrying in that direction. Bob followed, and then everything happened so quickly that they had no time to react at first.

The wild-eyed man in the bloody suit launched out of the darkness of the living room and grabbed them both, hurling them to the floor. Susan landed hard and Bob hit his head on the wall, momentarily stunning him. The man wrested the knife from his hand, reared back and stabbed down at Bob, who managed to twist his body away just in time for the blade to plunge into his side instead of his heart.

With a cry of pain and every bit of strength he had, Bob sat up and punched the man in the face. With a growl of anger, the man stood up and kicked Bob in the head, sending him sprawling.

Now Susan was on her feet, coming at the man with her own knife. He turned to face her, and shock stopped her as she saw his face.

"George . . . ?" her voice quavered in disbelief.

"Susan," he intoned, and she came at him with the knife but he grabbed her wrist and wrenched it hard, and the weapon flew from her grasp. She slapped him hard with her free hand, and he slapped her back with a force that sent her back down to the floor.

She looked up in terror as he stood over her, his eyes full of a mania she had never seen before. "Susan," he said in a voice that didn't seem human. "I want you. I want you so much. And now I have you . . . "

He dropped to his knees, straddling her. She

scratched at his face, and he grabbed her arms and forced them down and pinned them under his legs. Struggling to free herself, she screamed again as he said, "I've waited so long to have—"

*Bang!* One of George's eyes exploded out of his head, followed by a stream of blood. His body suddenly went limp on top of Susan, and she clambered out from under him as he fell to the floor, a gaping hole in the back of his head.

Looking up, she saw C.J. standing across the room, holding a rifle in his hand, the rifle that was mounted in the upstairs den, the one that she hadn't even thought was loaded. As he dropped it to the floor and ran to Susan, her first thought was a strange one: *Who taught you how to shoot that?*

\*\*\*

Dawn broke over the house as Bob was wheeled on a gurney over to an ambulance, Susan by his side. Two police cars sat in the yard with lights flashing, along with a van from a local news station. Half the cops on the scene were simply trying to hold the reporters at bay and control the growing crowd of onlookers as others investigated inside.

The bodies were laid out on the ground, covered in sheets, awaiting the coroner's van. Chief Cotter had uncovered George's face, and he looked grimly up at Susan as she passed.

As the attendants stopped the gurney and made ready to load Bob in, he saw George and said weakly to Susan, "Who was he?"

"He's my husband," she said softly. "Or was."

"He . . . what . . . ?"

"I'll explain it all to you later," she said, and then he was lifted into the back of the ambulance. She was just glad he was still conscious, that George hadn't

# NIGHTMARE

killed him the way he had killed poor Kathy and her boyfriend, and likely Tony and Candy as well. And almost killed C.J. How could it be George who did this? How could he be back as suddenly as he had disappeared nine years ago, leaving her and the kids alone? How had he become this . . . monster?

She knew the answers would come later. Right now, her concern had to be for her son. She looked over to the police car where C.J. sat in the back, being kept away from the reporters and anyone else who might disturb him, an officer standing beside the vehicle. C.J. seemed to be handling it all remarkably well, though she knew it would take him a long time to recover. And she resolved that she was going to do whatever she could to help him.

Behind her, a car raced up and skidded to a stop. Jackson and Dr. Williamson got out as Daniels ran up to greet them.

"Is it over?" Jackson asked Daniels, who replied, "Yeah. It's all over."

They pushed their way to the front of the crowd, and Dr. Williamson stopped short as he saw George lying on the grass, his eye socket destroyed. "Jesus Christ," he muttered. As Chief Cotter covered George's face back up and stood, Dr. Williamson asked him, "How many dead?"

"Here? Two, plus one who barely made it. But we're pretty sure he killed at least two more. You a reporter?"

"No, I'm—"

Jackson raised an arm, silencing Dr. Williamson. "We're just concerned citizens."

"Well, back up and show your concern over there, please," Cotter said, motioning them to join the rest of the bystanders.

They did, and Jackson kept going, motioning for Dr. Williamson to follow. "Come on. We've seen enough."

"I need to find out—"

"Let's *go*." Jackson pushed him, and Dr. Williamson had no choice but to go along. He didn't think they had seen enough. There was a lot more to be learned about what had gone on here. And he knew with growing dismay that a lot of other people were going to learn about it too.

In the back of the police car, C.J. saw the two men in suits weaving away through the rest of the crowd, who were in street clothes, a few of them in pajamas. He wondered vaguely who they were, since they stood out from the rest of the group.

Had the suited men wanted to talk to him? A lot of people had seemed to before they put him in this car. Now he was stuck in here and couldn't get out because there were no handles on the doors. It was like he was a criminal.

But he wasn't a criminal, he was a hero. Someone had said that before he was led to the car. And that person had been right. He *was* a hero. He had saved his mom's life. Not Bob or the police, but him. He had forced his way out of that closet and gotten the rifle off the wall and found the shells he knew were in the bureau beneath it, and stopped that man from hurting his mom. He had killed him when no one else could.

And it had felt *good*, because not only was the man attacking his mom, but something told C.J. that he was also the one who killed Tony. So he was getting revenge for his friend too. There was something immensely satisfying and exciting about that feeling. And on top of it all was the sense of *power* he had when he pulled the trigger, and saw that his aim had

# NIGHTMARE

been perfect and the shot went right through the bad man's head. He'd been so scared right up to the point when he fired the rifle, but once he did, he felt exhilarated. He still felt it now.

He hoped it would last, and if it didn't, he wondered how he might be able to experience it again . . .

# EPILOGUE

**J**ACKSON STOOD UP as Cooper entered his office. It was once again nighttime, after everyone else had gone home, but at least Cooper had knocked this time.

There were no formalities. "Is the new subject in place?" Cooper asked.

"Yes. We begin the new drug trials tomorrow."

"And he's secure where he is?"

"He's not locked up, if that's what you mean. But there is more surveillance. You have nothing to worry about."

"That's what you told me before."

"Before, we were dealing with a man who had a history of seriously fucked-up violence. This guy has never hurt anybody in his life. And won't . . . until we tell him to."

"Until *we* tell him to. You get him conditioned, Jackson, and we'll take it from there. How long do you think?"

"It's hard to say. According to Dr. Lee, his trauma is still manifesting largely as guilt, with his desire for vengeance subsidiary at this point."

"That's because he has no one to direct it toward. They never caught the killer, isn't that right?"

"That's right."

# NIGHTMARE

Cooper nodded. "You and Dr. Lee bring that thirst for revenge to the forefront of his psyche. We'll give him a target."

"Targets, I'm assuming."

"You leave that to us. And make sure Dr. Lee keeps him under closer supervision than you gave Tatum."

"Like I said, that situation won't happen again."

"It had better not. Keep in mind, the fallout didn't touch you only because I didn't allow it to."

"Which I appreciate."

"And because Dr. Williamson was there to take the heat."

"Yeah. Poor bastard."

"He'll be fine. A man of his experience will land on his feet. Somewhere. Don't concern yourself about him. Stay focused on this subject. We're expecting results soon."

"You'll get them, I promise."

"Good. Deliver for us this time, Jackson, and the rewards will be plentiful."

Jackson smiled on the inside. He was indeed grateful that Cooper had protected him in the aftermath of the Tatum fiasco, and that Paul had been the one to lose his position. The guy had meant well, but Aaron Lee seemed more capable and assured, and like more of a team player. And the new patient was going to give them far less trouble. Jackson was sure of it.

\*\*\*

Jeremy Hayes lay in his bed, hoping the nightmares wouldn't be too bad tonight. He had been moved into the new facility just a few days ago, and the unfamiliar surroundings weren't helping his sleep.

The dream always played out the same way, as if

some malevolent force inside him was reaching into his memories and tormenting him with them. He walked down the stairs into the bowels of the theater, and called out Lindsey's name. At this very point she was still alive, the beautiful, vivacious girl who had stolen his heart the way no one ever had before. When she didn't reply, he approached the ladies' room to see if he could catch a glimpse of her without actually going inside.

And he did catch a glimpse of her—of her shoes, covered with blood. A dreadful force compelled him to the door of the stall, and he opened it and he first saw her legs, then her violated stomach, and finally her face. Her eyes.

That's what sent his psyche spinning into a dark chasm of utter despair—the sheer terror and hopelessness in Lindsey's eyes. He knew that her last thoughts had been of him, wondering why he had taken her to this place to die, and why he wasn't there to rescue her from this vicious, horrible fate.

It was his fault she was dead, his fault that she had been cruelly stolen from her family and the world. He had been told that it wasn't, that there was nothing he could have done, that it was just an awful, random crime, that God works in mysterious ways. He knew better, though, and the dreams came with regularity to remind him.

He wished that they had at least caught the fiend who did this, so they could be punished. More than that, he wished that *he* could catch the perpetrator, to make them suffer the way Lindsey had suffered, the way he was suffering now. But the killer had so far gotten away with it and would likely continue to do so, and there was no way Jeremy could possibly find him. There was no person he or anyone else could tie to

# NIGHTMARE

Lindsey's murder, no face he could imagine confronting to wreak any kind of vengeance.

There was only himself, and his own responsibility, and that's what consumed his mind. That's what slithered into his sleep to make him relive that terrible experience night after night after night. Seeing Lindsey dead over and over again.

Seeing her body. Her face. Her eyes.

*Her eyes . . .*

# ABOUT THE AUTHOR

Michael Gingold is a longtime horror journalist (for *Fangoria*, *Rue Morgue* and others) and novelization enthusiast, and an award-winning creator of Blu-ray documentaries and featurettes. His previous books include the *Ad Nauseam/Ad Astra* series and *The FrightFest Guide to Monster Movies*.